Rain

DEVAN ARNTSON

ISBN: 978-0-578-86460-0

Contents

RAIN

The Giant

Now the Army of the West was gathering for battle. Under streamers of purple, the rebels made camp behind the walls of an ancient, ruined fortress. The ruins of Farfair Hold were nestled in the crook of the Red Mountains. These mountains and the Dusk Hills below made up the Highlands, one of ten great regions in the Greyland Realms. Thousands of rebels milled around in their chainmail and steel helmets, acquiring arrows from fletchers and spears from smiths. Their tents pitched against the old rocks and in between dark ruined walls. Mountains towered over the valley in a bowl around them. The Army of the West stood guard in their camp, back against the high rocks.

To the East was their only chance of escape. Yet a league away, on the far side of the valley, stood rows of steel-plated knights. With a camp of their own. Each knight armed a shield with their family coat. Banners flew in the wind. Banners of red and gold, the Army of the King.

"Form ranks!" A captain yelled from the top of his horse. He held a tall banner in his hand. It shook as the wind swept down the mountains and across the valley.

"We've pushed them into a corner, men. Let's finish them off!" Another shouted as he rode back and forth in front of the men of arms.

On top of crumbled towers of the fortress, wizards prepared themselves. In pairs, they conjured fire to be launched towards the enemy. This was the first attack of the battle known as Three Mile March.

Members of the royal army looked up as the mid-day sky filled with light. An explosion shook the ground as fire crashed into the earth. Burning sulfur and fire rained down on the knights as they scrambled in the encampment behind the lines. The King's men took up their shields and ran for cover behind boulders and ruined walls. Their tents were consumed in the flames. Bits of fabric fluttered in the air with the rising smoke.

"Ready for advancement! Reform the line!" A royal knight ordered to the soldiers. His cape was long and red as the sky that fell on them. He had greying hair and a strong bristled chin. "Take up your arms!" Sir Ulfer hollered.

"Will we not retreat?" A soldier shouted through the chaos and the roar of flames.

"No," Ulfer pulled the solider by his breastplate. "We cannot retreat. This may be our last stand against these filthy rebels! We need to get the archers into firing range."

"Yes sir!" The soldier ran as the ground around him shook with meteor impacts. He found his shield and went to pick up a fallen comrade. Others hastily found their swords and bows and rallied again to begin to charge across the high valley.

"March forth!" A captain ordered. The plated soldiers made themselves into walls of steel as they stepped across the earth which caught fire behind them. Now there was no escape for either side. One army stood against mountain, the other, flame. Their only option was inevitable collision. Horsemen ran past the foot soldiers and formed charge. With spears and lances, they rode toward the rebel camp. A comet of fire crashed down and scattered a few of the stallions; bucking their riders off and fleeing away from the battlefield. Yet out of the fiery smoke, the other horsemen kept their charge.

"Wizards hold!" Orders came up from the camp to the towers at the base of the mount. The exhausted mages collapsed onto the rocks. Their cloaks scorched from the intense heat their magic produced. Their hands red with burns. "Archers, keep that calvary away!"

"What are we to do?" A rebel captain went into the war tent. Other officers stood around an elderly man, who was dressed in black, his face concealed with a hood. All looking to this aged man for an answer. "Our wizards cannot hold them. By the time they're rested enough for a second assault, the King's army will be at hand. If we do not advance, they will crush us against the rock."

"I know what the King's men will do!" The elderly man snapped. "Pull the forces uphill," He turned to order one of the men. "Climb the mountain."

"Sir," The armored officer put his helmet on and left the tent to promptly follow the order given.

"You two," The old man pointed to the next closest officers. "Get Gath."

"Sir?" One gasped, the other too mortified to speak.

"I said get the giant! Send it out to meet the King. His folly will accept the duel and give us time to fortify ourselves up the rock. With any luck, the giant will kill the King for us," He turned his back on the officers.

They scurried out of the war tent and made their way through a mob of soldiers retreating further back into their corner. Chain shirts pinged and chimed against itself as their wearers hurried to move and gather their supplies. Camp was being hollowed out, but the tents and fires remained among the dark stone walls and arches. The two officers in their purple surcoats, pushed against this flow of rebels to the far end of their camp. There, they drew near to the mouth of a cave. Iron bars were bent out of the rock where they might have once held something back.

"Is it still in there?" An officer asked one of the five guards posted at the entrance.

"Yes, sir. It hasn't left since we arrived," The guard spoke as the one officer proceeded into the cave.

"Alright. Fortify yourselves up the hill," The other officer waved the guards away. "Go!"

"Gath?" The first officer called into the shadows, his voice echoing off the dark rock. "Come out!" The officer trembled as the blackness in front of him began to shift. He walked backwards out of the cave as the dark mass followed.

"What... Do... You... Want...?" The shadow's voice bellowed. The officer looked up at the giant and stood firm.

"We have a task for you," His mouth quivered as he turned to point across the battlefield. "Go, take your sword and kill their King."

"Kill... The... King...?" The mass stepped forward, shaking the solid ground beneath them. The first part of the giant to reach the light was a sword of solid bronze. It was nearly the height of a man and shone like amber against the sky. For the crude giant that wielded it, this sword was of fine craftsmanship. "Kill... The... King!" Behind the sword followed a creature of enormous stature. Gath the Giant stood as tall and as broad enough to fill the cave. The creature doubled a man's height and its mane alone could cover a royal horse. The rebel soldiers and officers retreated as Gath picked up momentum with each step. Running out of the mountain side and passed the ruins, Gath stood in the center of the large open field.

The horses that were at attacking speed with readied spears all halted in fear of the sight before them. Their riders cowered at the creature. Their horses kicked and staggered. The calvary immediately pulled back to join the footmen and their captains.

"King!" Gath demanded as he stood as a lone tower in the valley. "Where is... King?" The giant roared as he looked out over the immense army before him. He waved his sword, pointing at each of the men in formation. The soldiers and knights of the royal army stopped and looked to one another. The riders on horses galloped back and forth in front of the battalions of men. "Where… is… the King?" Men looked around for him. Sir Ulfer stared straight ahead in fear for him, hoping the King would not be found.

"Does the Army of the West send out a borrowed champion?" A call hushed the ranks. His voice was even enough to silence the crows that lived on the mountains. Moving to the front of the lines, a man in bright armor appeared. His cape was flowing red and the crown on his ginger hair was gold with silver decoration. His shoulders and chest filled his grand suit of armor.

"Do they know who they have challenged you to fight? Do you for that matter? I am King Gabel the Strong. I have fought with lions and beasts. I rule the grandest kingdom in all the Realms! The King who knows the name of his God!" The King unsheathed his glistening sword that shone silver like the moon.

"Tiny king… Curse your god… I… Kill you both!" Gath mocked and raised his weapon. Gabel walked past his army and stood alone in the field with the giant. His flowing red cape brushing over the tall grass. The beast had made armor for itself using trunks of mighty trees as shin guards and thick hides as a skirt and bracers. It wore a necklace of skulls from horses and men that the giant had eaten.

"Adonai help me," Gabel adjusted his grip on the hilt of his sword. "Men, march onward! By the time you reach me, I will have vanquished this foe," Gabel ordered, not taking his eyes off the giant.

Gath rushed forward, his feet thundering the ground. He brought down his heavy sword, slicing into the earth; the King jumping out of the way in time. Gabel lunged where the beast's leg was exposed. Taking the bronze sword out of the ground, Gath swung in circles. Gabel ducked under the sweeping weapon and again attacked at the backs of Gath's legs, where his armor did not protect. The giant hollered in pain, stopping his spin, he swiped at Gabel in a flurry. Again and again, the giant brought across his weapon. Gabel tried to block with his own sword, but the force of his enemy blew the King's weapon out of his hand. As Gabel scrambled for his weapon, his army was walking closer. Armor clanked in relative unison as the regimented knights kept time in their steps, advancing on the enemy.

"Get the wizards ready," The cloaked old man ordered his officer from their hiding spot in the mountain.

"Sire, they're still a ways off."

"Do as I say!" The old man snapped. "They will learn soon enough that their shields cannot withstand fire."

Gath slashed across at the King, who swung his own sword to parry the attack. With two hands, Gath brought his sword over his head and chopped downward. Gabel held up his sword; one hand on the hilt and the other supporting the flat side of the blade. The two swords rang on impact, but Gabel remained steadfast. Pushing up, the

King threw Gath's sword back, then immediately slashed at the giant's hand. Gath roared and dropped his weapon. Gabel then charged, sticking his own sword through the creature's gut. Gath fell to his knees and clawed and grabbed at the King. With draining life, the giant crawled towards him, unable to retrieve his sword. Gabel rolled to the side and with two hands, grabbed Gath's bronze sword. The end of the bade was still on the ground as Gabel merely raised the hilt. Turning and stepping forward, the King brought the sword into an overhead swing and sliced the giant between the shoulders. Gath's head dropped to the ground at the foot of one of the soldiers. The King's army had just reached him. Gabel dropped the bronze sword and drew his own again. He raised it to show victory over his enemy, warning the Army of the West not to oppose his kingdom. The rebels in purple shuttered at the sight, but the cloaked man pounded his fists against the boulders in rage.

"Fire down on them! Burn them all!" He yelled, the old man's voice echoing from the mountain. The King's knights below looked up to see flames igniting from the high peaks.

"They're in the cliffs!" Sir Ulfer warned. With that, the fire came down.

"Run them into the mountain!" Gabel ordered as he retrieved his own weapon and led the sprint towards the enemy camp.

The mages on the cliffs could no longer produce flames for their hands shook with such fear as the King's army tore through their camp and ran up the walls of the mountain. Archers fired up and down the cliffs, but most rebels turned to run. They ran into the cliffs, through passes and into caves to escape the army of the King. Most however, were slaughtered against the rocks. And in that day, the knights of King Gabel thoroughly destroyed the Army of the West. Gabel had beaten the malicious rebellion.

After the battle was won, healers and priests from the royal army came and recovered their dead and wounded. Soldiers looked for their fallen brothers or fathers. A man with a tall, crooked staff went up to the King.

"Ezemiah," Gabel greeted this holy man.

"Terrible loss of life today."

"Let us hope that it's for a greater tomorrow. One without these dark and twisted magics. Perversions of the gift that's been given."

"Adonai be with you, my King. I hope, as well, this is the end of the war. The brothers will take the dead and prepare them for burial. Unless any special requests are made, they'll all be buried in Sanctuary."

"Thank you," Gabel nodded, exhausted from battle. The man with the staff went back into the valley and walked among his fellow monks who were loading fallen soldiers, from both armies, into carts to be buried. From the scattered bodies, a weapon that shone of amber caught his eye. Ezemiah walked over to the great bronze sword that lay next to its wielder.

"Brother, a hand," One of the monks called to him. Ezemiah turned then to help his fellow monks.

As the years went by, no other army had risen up against the King. The sons and daughters of the rebellion were left to work in poverty. The Realm of the West was hollowed out of their men and money, having spent everything. The other realms refused to trade with the West, crippling their way of life. The magic renaissance collapsed, and the great schools were abandoned. The people were forced to farm the rocky ground and fish their treacherous coast for food.

In the meantime, King Gabel grew old on the throne; his lords and knights under him quickly putting an end to those who rose up from the remnants. Years went on and the Kingdom once again flourished. Peace and prosperity covered the Realms. Guards that were stationed in the West were eventually called back and the rebellion was nearly forgotten.

The Dragon

East of the Red Mountains and passed the royal capital, was a deep wild land. Where trees grew thick and the vines and the brush covered everything like a green cloth. The realm of the Avarwood, as it is known to this day, covered much of the Southeastern portion of the continent. Where mighty trees creaked and whistled to each other as they swayed in the soft winds. Streams and grey stones marked this untamed forest as natural borders for the forest folk. Plant creatures, Beastfolk, fairies, and even the Ones of the Wood lived here with the force of nature itself as their only ruler.

Fields of clover dotted the ground between villages of tiny mushrooms and forests of ferns. Leaves rustling and birds calling was often the only sounds that could be heard in this sleepy corner of the Greyland Realms. The first colors of fall, green and gold, dyed the sunlight peering into the underbrush. Trickling rivers, soft wind, and falling leaves made the Avarwood truly a peaceful place.

Two hooded riders crashed through the bush. A knight on a pale horse swiftly followed. The cloaked men beat their horses with haste to gain distance from their pursuer. The animals snorted as they ran. They whipped through the vines and the saplings of the wood. Swerving seamlessly in between the birches. The knight leaned with his horse, dodging the oncoming branches.

The two reached a cobble road and sharply turned onto it. The lone knight soon to follow, his deep blue cape shook in the wind. His visored helmet left on slits for his eyes to navigate through the wood. Yet, by the time he reached the road, the riders had already disappeared into the mist.

The knight scoffed in frustration, turned his steed around and trotted back to where he knew his village was. The road was fair and white, moss grew in thick clumps in between the flat cobblestone that paved the way. He rode to the village of Thundertree. A little hamlet that was nestled like others within the forest. As he drew near, another knight was walking out to meet him. He was older in age, with dirty braided hair that fell gently onto his worn-out breastplate.

"Blast your stubborn vigilance!" He said to the knight. "The brigands stole no more than a few coin's worth of produce. Nothing the farmers can't replace. And what? Did you expect to chase them out to Maple Mountain?"

"Even further if I needed to," The knight dismounted his horse, chuckling. He removed his helm, to reveal his strong, young face. Fair skinned, light curls, and dark eyes. "Besides, there must be some man in this town who is vigilant. We certainly know your eyes are growing old."

The young knight led his horse past the older man, who at this time was aghast by the knight's comments.

"No way to talk to your mentor," Remus coughed before turning to walk back into the village. The two passed under the arch of a stone wall, the portcullis raised up from the ground. There were two other walls like it that guarded each road leading into town. Guards stood on top between the ramparts.

"You ought to be careful, though lad. The world is more dangerous than you. Vigilant or not," Remus said.

"Would you consider me dangerous?"

"Reckless more like. There's yet anything come from Thundertree that is *dangerous*."

"Be careful what you say now. My habits might be seen as a reflection of my teacher."

"Bah," Remus waved. "Nonsense. People know me as chivalrous around here. I keep those who keep the peace."

"Is that so?"

"I keep my eye on you, don't I?"

Now, Thundertree was large compared to the other villages that lay scattered across the Avarwood. A stone keep and a statue of Sir Thundertree, himself stood in the town's center. Its folk lived humble lives and made a living off of couriers and tradesmen that would pass through from the coastlands on their way to the royal capital of Castle Rock. The market was a circle around the town's statue. Green and white pennants were strung from each shop cart. Most of the village still being highly decorated from the late summer shamrock festival which marked the beginning of the harvest season. The village was under the watch of Lord Falren and his men. He lived a rather luxurious lifestyle in his keep, thus his men, the knights of the town, kept the order.

Falren was Lord of the whole Avarwood. Any village in the forest was under his rule and tax. Like most lords, he put his money forward into roadways and defenses for his towns. He didn't hoard his money, but Falren wasn't the most generous of lords either. He had a reasonable storeroom full of gems and gold coins, and the people knew it. Falren made sure to keep his subjects just satisfied enough so they wouldn't storm his keep. Otherwise, he spent his income on expensive wines, shipped all the way from the Blackrock Bluffs, north of the capital.

"Alack! Sir Delwyn has returned from yet another wild goose chase," Remus announced as he walked back to the stables where the other knights were discoursing. The young knight hung his head and smiled to himself as he walked past his brethren, leading his steed back to its stall. He tied it up and went back to his kin.

"Perhaps the reason Delwyn spends his hours chasing crooks," Taylor, one of the knights, put his arm around Delwyn. He was taller than Delwyn and had short, gingered hair. "Is because he is no good at chasing women!" The congregation of knights roared in laughter. The two knights exchanged shoves and then engaged in wrestling each other to the ground. The crowd was steadily amused by this charade, for it was common among several of the younger knights.

"Alright," Remus stepped in. "You don't want to become worse than the ruffians, now do we?"

"No, sir," Delwyn said.

"No, sir at all," Taylor chuckled as he wiped his bloody nose.

"Good. Now clean yourselves up before supper. Clean your horses before that."

"I thought when we became knights, we wouldn't have to do page work anymore," Taylor complained. "We never hear of great royal knights cleaning after their horses."

"Aye, traditionally. But there's no mother in the realm that would trust their sons to you heathens. You still roughhouse like boys; you get errands like boys."

"Oh, come on Remus," Delwyn said. "Just earlier you were saying I was the only one around here to take my job seriously. Too seriously, in fact."

"I would humor your argument, lads, but you know there's no one else who's going to clean up your horses. Even us old folk take care of our steads."

"Except your backs are all gone so as we still have to bend down and scoop all the shit," Taylor laughed.

"Watch your tongue or you'll be washin' it. Last I checked vulgarity isn't in our Code of Chivalry."

"Neither is cleaning up horse shit, but here we are."

"And obeying those in authority?" Remus asked.

"Come on Remus…" Taylor smirked as he tried to give the old man puppy eyes.

"That might have worked as a child, but you've grown up far too ugly for that now," Remus pointed at him and walked away. The knights erupted in laughter again.

That evening, the knights gathered in the great hall of the keep, where they feasted together as a family would. They feasted on lamb and other harvested foods. The hall was lit up by flame light that flickered from the candles and hearths along the wall. Sounds of the quiet village came softly through the pane windows, sounds of the blacksmith's hammer, sounds of the horses along the road. Large arches held up the roof and lead into the throne room. Blue banners hung from the walls. Where, at no one's surprise, lord Falren was not present. He was in his quarters, in a drunken haze.

The knights reveled stories of their travels over the dining table. They talked of great battles, of strange people from the far corners of the Realms, and of terrific monsters that had been vanquished. They too drank wine and enjoyed fellowship with each other.

"Dragon!" A large door flew open, which led outside. The wooden door echoed through the hall. A guard ran in, with the look of absolute horror. "A-a dragon has been spotted from the watchtower!" A large blaze erupted and became visible through the great stained windows of the hall. The heat could be felt through even the thick stone walls.

"Blasted, sound the alarm!" Remus said as he sprang to his feet. Soon after, loud bells could be heard ringing from atop of the keep. The rest of the court was up and moving to the armory. The men grabbed their swords and kite shields, which were mounted on the wall. They fastened on their helmets and bracers, the knights already wearing their chainmail and surcoats. Only the roar of fire and the clanking of steel could be heard.

"Advance!" The knights burst out from the main doors out into the village, shields at the ready. A green monstrosity was already laying waste to the market, it crawled on its four legs and took up the entire square. It crushed the statue of their patron knight under its tail. Several farmers had attempted to hurl pitchforks at the dragon, but its scales were only scratched. The beast gave out a terrible roar and retaliated against its foes and bit down at them.

The knights charged toward the dragon. They made a wall with their shields as the moved uniformly. "For Thundertree!" The men chanted out as they broke formation, sprinting at the dragon. Its piercing eyes locked in on the men. The dragon stood back on its hind legs and exhaled a ball of fire which came crashing down on them. The heat burned through several men's shields and ate at their flesh. The dragon came back down to its forefeet, crushing the men who were already burning. Several guards came up behind the dragon but were met by the whip of its tail that sent the men flying back, hurdling into the wooden stalls.

At this time, peasants and village folk were trying to flee from their homes, but the dragon drew a wall of flame with its breath and had captured them all within the village. Horses shrieked from the burning stables. The dragon heard its prey and drove its head through the roof. The beast bit down on a horse and brought it into the air. In a few bites of its jaw, the horse was swallowed whole.

Archers from the town's walls brought forth their arrows which fell on the dragon like hail. Some sunk into the beast's long neck. It flinched in pain and took flight, spreading its massive wings. The air against the ground kicked up dirt and pushed the men backwards. The air only fueling the flames even more. The dragon then swooped at the archers, clawing them with its talons. It landed on the wall; the weight of the dragon crushed the simple stones as it did so. The arch collapsed, blocking the road. Several of the guards came up behind it and sliced at its rear. The dragon thumped its tail, knocking several men off of the tattered wall. it then leapt off and back toward the center of the village, to where Delwyn took up his sword and ran to slice at one of the emerald legs. He pierced it, but with the jerk of its claw, Delwyn was thrown back into a hut that had already caught ablaze, like the rest of the village. He struggled to sit himself up. A log that was supporting the ceiling collapsed on him, knocking him unconscious.

Sir Delwyn hacked as he awoke. He lay covered in thick peppered ash, with embers still illuminating the village at dusk. The ash still fell like snow, the sky clouded with smoke. The town was still. No one had appeared to be alive. He pushed the fallen logs off of him and sat up. Smoke and ash were the only remains of his village. He let out several coughs, surveying the ruins as he did. The dragon was not in sight. He brought himself up to his feet, removing rubble from his path to get down to the road. He wore a grim, solemn look as he saw the crumbled statue of Sir Thundertree.

It dawned on him that all he knew and loved was lost. He staggered to where he knew his comrades had fallen. He found the body of Remus; he had been crushed into the earth. The old knight lay, holding his sword over his chest. When Delwyn saw this, he fell to his knees and wept. He later drew himself together and took from Remus' blue cape, a stripe of fabric and tied it around the hilt of his sword.

"I will keep this piece of you with me for as long as I have the strength to wield my sword," Delwyn said. He left the body and continued to the ruins of the keep. There, lay a shield with the emblem of Thundertree. It was blue with a white pine tree embedded in the center. Across this shield was one scratch mark, which cut deep through the metal, but not enough to break it. Sir Delwyn lifted this shield and armed himself.

As he grew nearer to the keep, he felt a presence of danger. He peered into the ruins through one of the holes in the wall. In doing so, he saw the dragon within. It lay asleep in the great hall. Sir Delwyn's whole existence filled with rage. He stepped forward, but then caught himself.

"Not today, but I swear on all the bones before me, you will die to my hand," Delwyn muttered under his breath. He slipped away from the keep and went to the road, where he glanced at the old sign pointing to Castle Rock. He started out on the road which led to the capital. Delwyn knew the ancient code, that a knight in a time of aid could call upon the King.

He walked along the road that cut through the forest. His cape dragged behind him, stained white with ash. He gripped the hilt of his sword, sheathed in his belt, and let the weight of his shield pull his left arm toward the ground. Sir Delwyn walked till his legs could carry him no farther. He collapsed onto his knees, his armor clanking against the ground. When he woke again it was midday. The sun cooking his armor. Heat radiated from the metal filled Delwyn with images of fire. He sat up and scrambled to rip his helmet off. He pulled off his greaves, now removing the hot steel with his bare hands. Sweating, he shrugged the heavy chain shirt off of himself. He sat for a moment, panting with relief. Retying his scabbard around his tunic. Delwyn took the shield and rose to his feet.

He saw the road had become silent with activity. The towers of smoke were still visible from his ruined village and warned any traveler to steer clear. He noticed a deer standing not far off in the brush. The stag had large antlers and ate at the ferns below. Sir Delwyn stepped closer to get a better look at the animal. Something caught the deer's attention, which swiftly darted back into the forest. Delwyn looked around but saw nothing. It was said that only those of the forest know what lay in the forest. Taking his hand off the hilt of his sword, he sighed.

He put his blue cape on over his tunic and started to walk. The road stretched through many miles of woodland, over creeks and hills. He walked on the path for days, having to gather whatever berries he could find and drink any water way he came across. Making fires at night and keeping his sword close at hand.

The trees had already turned with the coming autumn. Amber, ochre, and maroon leaves colored the forest. Birches and maples filled the background with their brown and white trunks. These trunks creaked in the wind. Delwyn looked into the forest as it called, yet his fire didn't hardly give him enough light to see what was there. Even as the wind died, a creak continued to echo from within. With a crash, Delwyn drew his sword and turned. Stepping out from the base of a tree, was a creature with wooden bark for skin. Its feet were roots, its arms and hands were twisted branches. Its eyes glowed emerald. It crunched the bushes on the ground as it took heavy steps forward.

"The Ones of the Wood," Delwyn gasped and raised his sword. The plant creature formed the branches of its hand into a sharp point and lunged at the knight. Delwyn stepped to the side and swung his sword. The blade stuck into the wood like an axe hacking at a tree. Delwyn pulled to free his weapon but was hit from behind. Falling to the ground, the knight was stuck with a blow from the tangle on branches. The One of the Wood wrapped its wooden hands around the hilt of the sword and swung at Delwyn as he was getting to his feet. The young knight ducked under his blade, sweeping over him. The wooden mask of a face was cold as the creature attacked in a flurry. The creature sliced one of Delwyn's arms as he dodged from the continuous attacks.

Delwyn dove and rolled to his fire. He grabbed one of the burning logs and threw it at the One of the Wood. It screeched at the flame reaching upward. Delwyn took another log and drove it into the creature's torso. Its wooden skin caught flame and began to burn. The creature dropped Delwyn's sword and fell to its knees. The knight armed himself again and swung to strike the creature in the crooks of its neck. It screamed in the language of the forest. The flames consumed the beast and eventually it laid down and burned up to ash. Delwyn simply standing by, catching his breath as he watched the creature slowly die.

The Knights

As dawn broke through the roof of leaves in the forest and the sun's warmth could be felt again, Sir Delwyn woke to find the usually quiet side of the forest. He got up and walked along until the road came to a hill, where the forest dropped off to reveal a vast plain. The centerpiece of this rolling land was a mountain, on top was a great white palace. A city built of grey stone was below it. The many buildings seemingly spiraled down the mountain to the base. A tall statue standing out among the rooftops. Red banners waved majestically in the great wind. Farmsteads huddled around the outer walls of the city. The grey and white stone glistened in the dawn over the plains, gold with crops. Waterworks ran through the mountain side, creating a mote at the base around the outer wall. Rivers spread out like veins that filled the whole land.

"Castle Rock," The knight said to himself. Sir Delwyn proceeded down the hill and though the long fields of wheat and barley. He went up the road to the main gate, which was ever open. Across the archway hung a red banner with the crest of the King. It was a crown with angel's wings, which was in gold. Guards were on watch from atop the ramparts. As Delwyn walked across the drawbridge, he could hear music from the within the city. The smell of meats and fresh baked goods coming from the many market stalls and shops that seemed to be the life of this renowned city. Just beyond the gate was the great statue that could be seen from far outside the city walls. On a high ledge was built a marble statue of a soldier holding a spear. The top of his helmet was reaching over a hundred feet tall. The Watchman of the Realms, as it was called, stood as symbol of the King's protection over his kingdom.

Going up the streets, Delwyn passed by many creatures that filled the pathways. Elves, a few dwarves, humans, almost any race of people that could be found in the Realms lived here also. He passed shops that sold potions and brews in glass vials that came in many irregular shapes. He passed a blacksmith, who pounded away with his hammer, making tools and weapons. The path spiraled up the mountain on a gradual slope. Delwyn walked up the busy streets to an inner wall, where he was met by a guard.

"State your business, plebeian," The stationed guard called out to Delwyn, covering in soot and dirt.

"Nay, I beg your pardon. I am Sir Delwyn of Thundertree, a knight of my people. I am not some peasant," The knight responded with offense. The guard's face turned red with embarrassment. "Now, I ask that you open this gate, I have news for the King himself and it is of dire urgency," The sentry looked around as if to differ to another guard to take care of the situation. Delwyn coughed to regain the guard's attention.

"Right, I'll, uh... I shall open the gate for you, sir," The guard turned around, went to the gate, and unlocked with a rather large key. "Y-you may enter."

"Thank you for your... cooperation," Sir Delwyn rolled his eyes as he walked past the guard.

The white stone castle stood before him now. It was beautifully crafted. Many gardens stretched along the stairway that led upward to the main door. Banners like before soared over the towers on this grand fortress. Statues of angels and knights were placed among the lush rose gardens. This side of the wall seemed quiet, Delwyn saw no servants tending the grounds or any nobles roaming about, just he alone was in the courtyard before the castle. He arrived at the sally port, the main doors, and with a great push, they swung open.

The hall was majestic, unlike any building he had seen up to this point. Paintings were hung across the archways; paintings of great heroes and mighty battles filled the ceilings. Past Kings and knights on white horses all fighting beasts or armies of evil.

The hall was lit by chandeliers which were coated in a glistening silver. A long red carpet led the way into the castle corridors. Delwyn stepped inside and took this all in. The sights of the castle and its architecture had almost made him forget why he was here. Soon, though he snapped back to the weight of the situation. He proceeded down the great hall and into the throne room.

A tall, square cut marble throne was elevated from the ground. It was decorated with gold and red cushions. On it, sat High King Gabel the Strong. He was ruler of this land before Delwyn was born but was still fit in his age. His greying red hair was still full and his chin, like the rest of his face, was nearly sculpted from stone. He wore a gold crown with ornate silver which sat firmly on his head. Nobles were attending him, though they seemed to look concerned.

"Sir, if you would just lift the ban, then these rebels would stop rising against you," An old nobleman with a cane suggested.

"No, Grev. Then all of my men would have died for nothing," The King shot down.

"Would be a sign of weakness were we to back down now. So long after our victory in the Red Mountains," Another added. "I would say, it is rather odd we had another attack. After so many years of compliance."

"Surely," Another nodded. "To propose a lift of the ban would be weakness. Where is your house from, Grev? To the West?"

"No!" The old man shook his head, taken back by the accusation. "My house is from the East. As are my loyalties. I only advocate for peace. Such a simple correction to end decades of strife."

"Giving up punishment does not make their acts less evil. That is not justice," Gabel leaned forward on his throne. They murmured to each other and bickered with King Gabel, but all fell silent as Delwyn approached. The knight of Thundertree kneeled before his king, bowing his head in respects.

"Did that filthy guard of mine let you in here?" Gabel asked Sir Delwyn. His face was stern, as if Delwyn had interrupted a serious matter. The young knight bowed again and then proceeded.

"Aye, but I told him I needed to see you at once, it is-" Delwyn was cut short.

"I am afraid it will have to wait, son," The King stood up to leave his throne with the other noblemen. "Do escort yourself out."

Delwyn was caught speechless, dissatisfied with such lack of care.

"A dragon has burned my village to ash. I, as it were, am the only survivor," The young knight persisted. Gabel sighed and turned back. "I came here from the village of Thundertree, I am a knight among my kin. Now I have come to call on the King for aid, as is my right."

"I am sure that we can give you some compensation for your losses, however great. But there are more *pressing* matters at the moment that I must tend to."

"Your majesty, with all respects, it is the duty of the King to hear a call for aid."

"Enough! I am the High King of all the Realms; do you not think that I may have more important things to handle than the death of one dragon?" Gabel snapped. Delwyn stepped back in silence, his face flushed. "I am sorry for your loss, sir knight, but what I am dealing with is an issue the entire kingdom is facing. Aye, I have felt that urge for vengeance, but maybe you must put aside your anger to see the bigger problems in the world."

With that, the King left with his nobles quickly following. Sir Delwyn defeated, sat on the steps, which lead to the throne. He stared blankly at the floor, not knowing what to do next. It was not long after, the ancient looking nobleman returned.

"Get up, son," The elder gentleman said to him. Delwyn was startled out of his thoughtlessness. "Come on, the King's knights wished to see you. You may be of use to them."

Delwyn rose to his feet and followed the man. They went to a side door, which lead down into a lower corridor. There was a dining hall, and a hearth in the corner of the room, connected to that was a barracks where the knights of the castle lived. Those knights were collected in their dining hall. They argued loudly with one another. They did not notice Delwyn come down the staircase, for they were all too invested into their debate.

"This was a serious attack, not some measly crime!" One knight argued.

"Are you suggesting there's a coup waiting to happen? Some hidden army waiting to take power?" A redheaded man refuted.

The nobleman quietly went to an older knight who was at the head of the table, "Sir Ulfer, I have brought the man you asked for," The old knight nodded and turned toward Delwyn. The rest of the table caught on to these events and the commotion came to a halt, eventually they were all looking at Sir Delwyn.

"Thank you Grev, you may leave us," The knight waved. The nobleman bowed, then left them and proceeded back upstairs. "Come boy," Sir Ulfer motioned for Delwyn to approach the table. "We have been told that you survived a dragon attack. That is, by most accounts, an impressive feat."

Delwyn nodded, skeptically.

"Well, did you kill the beast?" Another knight shouted, one of the redheads.

"No. That is why I came here, to seek help to kill the dragon," The men at the table seemed disappointed in his answer.

"Ever slay any trolls?" Another knight questioned him. Delwyn shook his head.

"Any giants? Ogres?" Sir Delwyn answered no to all these questions.

"I am fairly young but am no less a knight of my village. On the journey here, I killed One of the Wood, if you've heard of those," Delwyn defended himself. Another man at the end of the table seemed very annoyed by all of this.

"Ulfer, all of you. Get on with it, we might as well give it to him straight," The knight hushed his companions. Sir Delwyn felt almost disturbed and confused by all that has been going on since he arrived in the castle. The man, who had short black curls turned to Ulfer.

"Very well, Igran…" Ulfer, the old man, sighed. "King Gabel's unwillingness to help is not because he does not wish to. Nay, it is because *we* are in need of help. Sit down, son. You'll be here some time. On the day before last, the

King's chambers had been broken into. Just earlier that evening the castle servants found poison in the King's wine. Now the whole palace is in a state of distress. Being one of the most secure fortresses in all the Realms, we've naturally become very worried. Whoever was behind these attacks is very powerful and poses a very serious threat to our kingdom. We conclude the job had been done by someone on the inside, someone who did not need to breach the castle. That is why you can be trusted, Sir Delwyn of Thundertree. You are a traveler, who has spent his whole life in his own village," Ulfer explained. "Look, son. We know you have a quest of your own, but we need all the good men we can get, they're in short stock. I am sure that if you stay and aid us in our fight, we would all take up arms in yours."

"You want me to help you? Help the King, that is," Delwyn asked.

"Yes," Ulfer said. "We'll honor your help in exchange for ours."

"That seems reasonable," Sir Delwyn replied.

"Good," Igran nodded.

"So, tell us about this dragon," One redhead spoke up.

"Ragnar..." Igran looked over at him.

"What? I want to hear about the beast."

"His whole village was just incinerated; you really think he wants to talk about it?"

"It's fine," Delwyn said. "It was green dragon. Been a few years since one's been seen in the Avarwood, not sure where it came from. Its fire was so hot, the sheer heat of its breath could melt a man's shield. Its razor claws could break apart stone. It ate a horse whole, snatched her right up from the stables. It trapped the whole village in its flames, took everyone.

"You have more than our respect, Sir Delwyn. Aye, if we are to get out of this mess, surely we shall help you avenge your kin," Igran said as he left for the barracks.

The men eventually all slipped into their racks in the bunk room. Delwyn placed his gear down next to an open bunk and fell in. He fell asleep quickly, as did the rest of the knights, none knowing what was to come.

Delwyn woke to the sounds of the castle coming to life. He strapped on his sword and washed his face in the water basin. His scratched the dirt out of his skin and poured some water over his hair. Igran, who seemed to be in charge of the select bunch, and his men were getting ready for their tasks ahead. Two redheaded men were arguing over which one of them owned a particular warhammer.

"That is Ragnar Stoneram," Ulfer pointed to the man who had his red hair tied in a braid yet shaved on the sides. "And that is his brother, Adir the Mighty," He stated as he pointed to the other man, who wore his hair down, which went down long enough to reach his admirable beard. "These men hail from the Northern Reaches, near the Ice Oceans. They are quite deadly in battle."

"How'd they end up here?"

"By the King's offer. In the great rebellion, we feared the West would start to influence the Northern Reaches. So, any clansman who agreed to fight for the throne was granted knighthood. They were among the only to survive."

Igran could be heard from the knight's dining hall, arguing with a servant. The two took their argument up the stairs into the great hall. He had black curls and always worse a serious look on his face.

"And what of Igran?" Delwyn asked.

"Ah, Sir Igran is a fine knight, if you can mind his temperament," Ulfer thought.

"Is he ill-mannered?"

"Well, no… His past has made him irritable. He grew up much like you. A knight of his village with a happy family. He was caught though in the crossfire of two very unstable people. He lived in a farmstead near the foothills of the Dawn Mountains. The land then was governed by a particular Lord Walden. The territory was natively owned by the orcs, but Walden was granted a claim on the land. Men grow dirty with greed, so Walden sent parties of men to overtake nearby orc camps, wanting to expand his territory. But the invaders stood no chance…

"The orcs, as you know, are a warring people. They did not react kindly. Clans from the mountains mustered to retaliate. In the dark of the night, the orcs descended on the land that Walden ruled over. The grounds and farmlands were set ablaze as the orcs marched to the lord's keep. Many villagers tried to run from the battle. Igran was defending those trying to flee, but he was not there when his wife was struck down."

"I had no idea," The young knight was at a loss for words.

"Don't worry about him too much. Like I say, he's a fine knight. Truly. Anyway, I think we're all expected upstairs."

They made their way up to the throne room, meeting several well-dressed individuals as they did so. Delwyn still wearing his dirtied tunic, felt out of place.

"This is Lady Evangeline, princess of this kingdom," Ulfer bowed, introducing the maiden. She was tall and had a thin build. Long brown hair flowed down to her lower back, which complimented her green eyes. Her dress was long and fitting, it was red with gold trimmings, the colors of the kingdom. On her head was a gold circlet with rubies.

"Please, Sir Ulfer, I am flattered, yet I do not need such fancy introductions," She turned to Sir Delwyn. "I do not believe we have met; I thank you for your services to my father," Delwyn bowed his head in acknowledgement.

"Now this is Prince Ivan," Ulfer chuckled. "He may be young in years, but he's as strong as an ox. Takes after the King in that regard," Ivan shook his head and chuckled with the old man. Ivan was fifteen, only a few years behind Delwyn. He always had on a black doublet which matched his dark hair. On the crown on his head, was a circlet of silver.

"We best be off your highnesses," Igran bowed to the pair of siblings. "We've work to be done yet, let us have no delay. Ragnar take Sir Delwyn to the potions shop in the markets. They may be able to identify the poison that was placed in the wine. Perhaps find out where it came from. Adir and I will do some investigating around the castle, see if anyone saw anything the night the King's quarters were broken into. Ulfer, I need you to look after these two," Nodding toward the prince and princess, "Their usual servants appear to be... elsewhere."

"You know I always have my eye on them," The old man nodded. He had helped raise them like a grandfather, even taught Ivan how to wield a sword.

"Good," said Igran.

Ragnar nodded and patted Delwyn on the back as he walked to the main doors.

"We might as well find you some new armor while we're down in the markets," Ragnar said as they walked down the street. "At least enough so you won't be vulnerable in battle. Perhaps replace that split shield of yours."

"The shield will hold up. But I could use the armor," Delwyn replied. They continued down the hill, Ragnar waving to the civilians who passed by. Most everyone knew who the royal knights were. Often finding themselves sorting out civilian affairs or helping anyone who called for aid. Between the brief greetings, Ragnar began to speak.

"I'll admit, lad. I'm nervous for what is to happen. No one goes after the King unless they are either out of their

40

damn mind or they are looking to take charge. Both of which could be a scary thought."

"I haven't been here a day. Trust me, I have no idea either," Delwyn admitted.

They passed by the many shops and went through several systems of alleyways until they found themselves at a shop called the Cracked Phile.

"Try not to touch anything, personally I don't trust any of this magic business and who knows what some of these potions might do," Ragnar cautioned the young knight.

The nook was filled with glass vials of many shapes, each filled with a different bizarre liquid. Each labeled with a different name which, more or less, told its property. The two walked up to the counter in the far back of the store. The shopkeeper was an elf, who was tall and had distinctly pointed ears. She wore simple and modest robes and an amulet around her neck.

"What can I do for you gentlemen?" She spotted the royal crest on Ragnar's armor. "I don't recall the King or any nobles ordering anything to be picked up."

"No bother, m'lady. We are here on more private business. We'd ask you keep this meeting between us," Ragnar leaned on the counter. She nodded. "Good. Now, we are wondering if you could extract and identify a poison."

"Sure," She said.

Ragnar pulled from his pocket a concealed phial which contained a sample of the tainted wine. He did not care to mention that it was the King's wine that was poisoned, for he did not want to raise suspicion. The elf reached across the countertop and received the flask out from Ragnar's hand. She uncapped the phial. Closed her eyes and hovered her open hand over the open container. Her hand began to tremble and soon a magic light fled from her palm and sank into the liquid. She lifted her hand, which directly raised the liquid from the phial. She held it in suspension in the air. With the flick of her wrist, the pool of liquid separated into two. One was the red wine; the other was a dark and sinister poison. The elf then took up another bottle and filled it with the poison, placing the wine back into its original container. The elven shopkeeper opened her eyes and refocused on her surroundings. The two men stood across from her, impressed by this mage's skill. She cleared her throat. Turning her attention to the vial of poison.

"Interesting..." She peered into the void of dark fluid. "This is a rather rare poison. Not one you would come across often," She turned from the counter and flipped open an old book. One which taught potions and ingredients. "This particular brew is very expensive. Whatever it was used for, it certainly would have been *important*," She glanced up at the men, with a slight look of discomfort. She proceeded further. "No shop in the city would have been able to make this. I suspect that it's user was very wealthy and came a long way to do... well, whatever needed to be done."

Delwyn and Ragnar exchanged glances.

"Any chance you know the origin of the poison? Or where the ingredients came from?" Ragnar asked.

"The ingredients would have come from all over the Realms. Like I said, very expensive to prepare. It could have been brewed anywhere."

"We thank you for your time, miss," Ragnar sighed as he turned from the counter to head back to the streets. Delwyn nodded, he grabbed the flasks as he turned to walk out as well. "Well damn, boy," Ragnar cursed as they exited the shop. A half dozen guards passed by them as they made their way back to the street.

"This was no simple assassination attempt. This could be a serious foreign threat. The kingdom, it's practically the whole Realms. Whoever did this wouldn't be bold enough to do it unless they had one hell of an army that could match ours," Ragnar scoffed at this. "No one had tried to take the throne since before the signing of the Royal Rock Treaty. To disturb the kingdom, well it would disturb the balance between all the races."

"You think it race has to do with it?"

"Well, I don't know for sure. But this kingdom stands for equality. Everyone is allowed to live and work here. I don't know why else someone would attempt something like this unless they wanted a drastic change."

Delwyn didn't reply. They walked in silence for a few minutes before ending up at the blacksmith's shop. The building was partially carved into one of the cliffsides, with the forge pushed back into a cave. Several smiths were working on the anvils and tending the storefront.

"Ragnar!" An orc from the back of the forge came out when he saw the knights. His skin was dark grey with sharp teeth and pointed ears. "Been awhile since you've visited my shop. You still owe me from that jousting tournament by the way."

"We both know this isn't your shop," He laughed. "How you doing, Kros?"

"Oh, fine," The smith replied. "What can I do you for?"

"This young knight needs some armor," Ragnar slapped Delwyn on the back.

"You sure you're strong enough to carry it?" The orc chuckled. "Course you are. Come on in, let's see what I have."

The orc told Delwyn to try on several breastplates until they found one that fit. He outfitted the knight with greaves and gauntlets.

"And lastly, your helmet," He gestured to his shelf, full of helmets of different styles. Great helms and sallets, all lined up on in the dimly lit shop. Delwyn grabbed one with a full visor like the one he used to have.

"This will do," He said.

"A fine choice. Should protect that pretty face of yours," The orc chuckled. Delwyn rolled his eyes and smirked.

"I can't pay for this," He said.

"Course you won't," Ragnar assured. "You're a knight of the King, now. He'll pay for it. We'll send someone down to cover the cost," He said to the orc as they started up the hill.

"Send down the gold you owe me!" Kos called after him, but Ragnar waved.

Sir Delwyn and Ragnar eventually returned to the palace. They went to another wing of the castle were the other knights, Adir and Igran, were eating lunch.

"Well, brother? What news of the poison?" Adir asked as Ragnar approached him.

"I am afraid, for it is not good news. The poison is rare and highly expensive. Aye, whoever dare used it had intended to replace the King. This was not some spur of the moment attack, but highly planned," The knight sighed as he told his brother the news. "I am unsure what is to come, but we can all make certain that this is only the beginning."

"Or the resurgence of an old enemy…" Adir reminded.

"What are we waiting for? We shouldn't stand by like this while someone is in the shadows plotting against the King. We should put whatever guards we have on high alert," Delwyn spoke up from across the dining hall.

"No! We cannot throw the people into a panic; we need to handle this with tact," Igran snapped. "We solve this subtly, and the people will never know."

"'Tis foolish, if we had more guards aware of the situation, then we would have more eyes on the lookout for this kind of activity," Adir stepped in, Igran glared at him across the table. "I just think-"

"Guards should be on the lookout of this activity, regardless of the present circumstances," Igran said.

"Pardon me for interrupting…" a soft voice came from across the hall. Princess Evangeline proceeded from the throne hall.

"My lady forgive us for our rage," Igran bowed at her arrival. The other knights too, did bow their heads at her royalty. With a sigh, he let go of his frustration. "What is it we can for you, your highness?"

"Please," Evangeline smiled softly. "I am only wondering where my father went, I had not seen him all day."

The men looked up at each other with the same worried expression. A grim chuckle came from a dark corner of the hall. Grev appeared from the shadows, looking wizened and mad. He began to rave, with his eyes flaming in hatred.

"You all were too busy running around to notice. Your King has fled. He ran off like the coward he is! Ran off with all the other nobles too afraid of this adversity."

"You lie," Evangeline stepped towards him, defending her father. "A King does not run."

"No?" Grev mocked her. "Where is he? He left you here, I am sure of it," His words hissed out through his clenched teeth. Ragnar charged at the old man. He gripped by the shoulders and threw him to the ground. His cane tumbling away.

"Where is the King?!" Ragnar demanded. Evangeline covered her mouth. Igran cared not to intervene. Ragnar pulled him up and stuck him against one of the pillars in the hall. "Where is he, you swine?!" The old man coughed as he chuckled at his attacker. Ragnar hit him to the ground with the back of his fist.

"Mercy," Grev coughed. "I will tell you where he is going," He old man sat himself up from the marble floor.

"He fled to Frostford. On the Western Coast. I overheard him tell his wealthier, more favored nobles," Grev turned and spat blood from his mouth. "He has a safehouse there," Igran slowly walked toward him. Although beaten, Grev still looked up with his crooked smile.

"I would suggest you take that ugly grin of your face, that is if you intend on keeping it," Igran drew his sword at pointed it between Grev's eyes. "How can we all be clear that you are telling us the truth?"

"If I'm not, you know where to find me," He chuckled as he brought himself to his feet. Igran kept his sword held out. "In the meantime, I have ordered for more guards. So, do feel free to search for the King. I will have everything under control here," At this time, Ulfer came from the other hall with Prince Ivan. Both were at shock to see what had taken place.

"Sir Ulfer," Igran turned his head, "You are to take care of the Prince and Princess while we are away. You have command of the guard since this *fiend* has lost his mind," Ulfer nodded in agreement, trusting there was reason behind his kin's orders. "The rest of us, we are going out to find our King," The rest of the knights went down the barracks to pack what supplies they happened to need.

"Sir Igran," Evangeline went to catch up with him. "Please believe me, my father is no runner. I will not have him disgraced this way."

"Nor will I, my lady," Igran turned back. "I fear he may be in danger. *That* is why we are going after him."

"You get him back. This kingdom needs her King."

"Yes, my lady," Igran bowed and went down the stairs to the barracks. "Ulfer, I will see you soon."

"Fare you well," Sir Ulfer said as he took Evangeline and Ivan up the tower to their chambers.

"I am unsure what is unfolding, but it has been my duty to guard you two since your births. I uphold that duty though all this. Ivan, you must be strong in your father's absence. Carry your sword at all times. Evangeline, you are so wise. Wise beyond your years. We need someone like you to have a good head on their shoulders and a good heart in their ribs. Your father, my King, will expect this of you both."

"What are we going to do?" Ivan asked.

"I'm not sure. But you listen to me above everyone else, you understand? We three trust no one. We don't know who

The Prophet

Elsewhere, King Gabel awoke with the sounds of horses and men along a trail. His head throbbed as he sat up. To his surprise, he found that he was tied to the back of a wagon. His sword and crown stashed away under other valuables that they had taken. The setting sun glaring in his eyes. One of the men took notice in the King's waking.

"By the time they find your corpse, it'll be far too late," He said to the King.

"Where are you taking me, you bastard?" The King's eyes lit with rage. "I am High King Gabel and even if you manage to vanquish me, my men will run you all into hell!"

"Maybe so, but soon enough your men will have to bow to the new king. Nay, if they are as foolish as you then they too, will be killed. Not far different from your noblemen."

The guard gestured toward another wagon, where the nobles of King Gabel's court lay dead. Blood pooled from their necks, seeping into their elegant robes. Gabel clenched his fists and pulled on the restraints with all his might. It was no use to him. The King eventually stopped struggling yet kept the same look of rage on his face. The detachment of guards came to a split in the road, which was marked by a post with signs that pointed in the direction of nearby towns. One of which pointed the way to the village known as Crossroads, the guards made each other aware of this sign and proceeded in its heading.

As they moved steadily up the road, the King caught a sense that they were being stalked. Movement could be seen in the pines that surrounded them. Shadows not lining with the trees, leaves not moving with the wind. A lone arrow came whizzing past one of the guards.

"Halt!" One of the guards commanded. They stopped the caravan, scanning the tree line for whomever fired the arrow. Another arrow came from behind and struck one of the guards in the spine. Gabel sank into his wagon, to take cover from the ambush. Soon, a voice could be heard from within the forest's shadow.

"Empty all your cargo and gold!" The voice demanded. There was a pause as the guards looked at one another.

"Or what?" One of the guards questioned.

"Or we draw blood from every one of you and take your belongings either way."

The guards unsheathed their sabers and aimed them arbitrarily into the forest. The few armored guards seemed a bit confident that they would scare off the highwaymen. Smirks were shared amongst the men as they waved their swords at the trees. Their great sense of pride was quickly shattered at the sound of men on horseback thrashing out of the pines and bushes, charging at them with swords of their own. The bandits had their faces concealed behind black masks and hoods. Horses snarled as their riders jabbed at one another with their swords. One of the guards was stabbed through the chest and fell off his horse, into the wagon where King Gabel was. He quickly reached for the man's saber, using it to cut his hands and feet free from the carriage. Clashing of swords was heard all around him. Gabel peered over the wagons edge to spot a bandit who had his back turned. He sprang out, throwing the bandit to the ground. Gabel adjusted himself on the saddle.

"Ya!" The horse was quickly turned around and King Gabel took off into the forest.

"Stop him," A few guards ran on foot after him, but were quickly outran. Soon after, the guards who didn't run away had been vanquished. The bandit who was thrown off his horse brought himself to his feet. He glared off in the direction that the King had taken off.

"Are you gonna help us loot these bodies or just stand there?" One of the other crooks said to him, as he was still examining the woods.

"Aye, I'll be there."

"Oi, look at this," One of the masked men took out Gabel's sterling sword. It was tall with inscriptions along the sharp blade. The crest of the King at the hilt.

"Should be able to sell some of this off in town."

Gabel traced his way back to the road sign the caravan had passed just before they had been ambushed. He was relieved to discover he was close to a familiar city. Kicking his newfound horse, Gabel took off along the intersecting road, heading north. He rode over the dirt and through the trees. Birds called and bugs flew between the greenery. He whipped his horse, running with haste toward his shelter. Riding past the Red Mountains, he saw the city come into view. In the valley to the Northeast of the mountain range, appeared steeples and farmhouses. Vineyards and orchards surrounded the buildings. Leaves of gold and green painted the valley. Larches and pines, maples and apple trees filled this place with color. Farmers with herds of sheep and cattle filled it with life. Walls and hedges surrounded the agricultural city. Farms stretched the entire meadow.

"Sanctuary. The City of the Prophets," Gabel said to himself as he took in the countryside. His horse galloped down the slope and deeper into the valley. The road twisted back and forth; rocks were stacked as retaining walls for each level of the road. Gabel rode down the mountainside and up the hills of the valley. He entered the village, passing between wooden fences and hedges. Farmers walked by on their way to the market. The air was filled with the scent of cooking meat and the burning of incense from priests. Bakeries and breweries added to the nice aroma of the town. Calls from vendors were mixed with oracles recited by the many priests. "Fresh pumpkins, get your squash!"

"And for the salvation of the Realm, our..."

"Roasted chops here!"

"…races were descendants of this one who walked the earth with and called them his own…"

"I'll take ten pieces for that!"

"His kingdom will come. He will take the shattered and make it whole again. Mending with gold…"

Apart from the market, there were wineries and other shops on either side of the road. Most walking about couldn't recognize Gabel without his crown. Not even his red cloak, insulated with white fur gave him away. Winding his way through the modest dirt streets, Gabel came to a walled monastery. A monk from on top the wall spotted him and ran down the simple watchtower to open the wooden gate. As Gabel rode through, it was shut again behind him. Robed monks tended the weary horse as the King dismounted.

"Your highness," The monk bowed.

"Ezemiah?" Gabel asked one who was sent out to greet him. Without a verbal reply, the monk turned and motioned for the King to follow. Gabel walked past the large stone temple and humble wooden houses built for each monk. Behind these structures was a wide vineyard, full of grapes being harvested. A tall winery could be seen on the far end of the vineyard. Gabel was led to the middle of the vineyard to a raised garden. Ten or so feet above the meadow, this small tower held many ferns and a single tree growing from the center. Stone stairs spiraled up to this garden, where another monk was working the ground. The short monk that was escorting Gabel gave a low cough to get the other's attention.

"My liege!" A man in brown and white robes stood and bowed slightly before Gabel. His long hood was off his head and rested along his back. His hair was light, with a long, aging beard as well. His eyes were tired with the man's calm composure. The other monk bowed and left the King and this man alone.

"What do I owe this visit? This is most unexpected."

"Ezemiah, I must speak with you in private," The King said, short of breath.

"This place is safe," The robed man assured. Looking around, Ezemiah knew he wasn't in hearing distance of any of the other workers. "What do you need my King?"

"The Army of the West is rising again. They did not all perish at Three Mile March."

"No," Ezemiah shook his head, knowing the truth. "No, I have seen their fire from the mountains. Their banners fly once again, yet they've kept in secret. They've been mustering in that wicked fortress they're trying to rebuild."

"Aye. And now they've infiltrated my court. I do not know among my knights or nobles, who is loyal to me. They attempted to poison me. When that failed, I was beaten and taken. They've killed the rest of my court."

"Where were they taking you?" Ezemiah leaned on his walking stick.

"West. If not to kill me there, then to get me out of the way for whatever is happening now at Castle Rock."

"So why flee here? It was not only for protection, was it?" Ezemiah asked.

"You are a man I can trust. I need your counsel."

"Go on."

"Please, Ezemiah, will we be blessed in battle?"

"What kind of question is that?"

"Is our God on our side or not?" Gabel asked earnestly.

"No…" Ezemiah sank his shoulders, thinking deeply. "Our God is on his own side. Only, you can choose to fight for him."

"If we do, though, what will become of the Realms?" The King insisted. Ezemiah sighed.

"Gabel, you are strong and righteous like no other King before you. You know the name of our God and have killed many dark things. But it will not be you who will vanquish all evil. There will soon come a time when your city is empty and silent," Ezemiah tried to assure his King while speaking what he knew.

"How do you know this?" Gabel looked intently at him.

"You come to the City of the Prophets and yet you ask where my knowledge is from?"

"So, there is no hope. Our God has shown you of my defeat already," Gabel turned away.

"I did not say that," Ezemiah corrected slowly. "There is a hope. You are still a protector of good. Yet you will not vanquish *all* evil, but there will come a King after you who will. There indeed will be a time when your castle is silent, but after you will rise a King who will fill the streets with singing. As righteous as you are, my King, *he* is the salvation of this kingdom."

"Have I then fought for nothing? How do you know this King will be any more righteous or mighty than I?!" Gabel turned and took a few steps away.

"My King, he will bear the name of our God," Ezemiah said sternly. The prophet's voice echoing over the vineyard in the valley. The King looked back to him. "He will be called Adonai."

"Do I surrender then? Let them come if I know I will not vanquish them?" King Gabel sat down on the stone bench, thinking of the implications of his defeat. Not knowing what to believe. "Years I have dealt with rebellion and pressure to let them have their way. Have I really fought, defended righteousness, for nothing?"

"No," Ezemiah said strongly, kneeling before the King. "No, you can still hold them off. Still win the day. But you no longer fight for your self-preservation. You must fight with faith in what you will not see. Fight knowing there will be salvation. Having the faith that the Realms *will* be saved from this evil. You must humble yourself in this, Gabel. If you say you are the King who knows the name of his God, then you must live in service to Him. As many now will fight for their King, you must fight for yours."

"And will your men fight with me?" Gabel opened his hands towards his friend.

"The knights here are not yours to will. You know that," Ezemiah sank.

"Then for what reason have they been called to fight under His standard? Will they fight on the side of their God? Will they fight for this King who will come after me, who bears the name of Adonai?" He asked. Ezemiah thought somberly and sighed.

"The Fervent would fight for him, yes. It would be their duty."

The Regent

Igran led the other knights out of Castle Rock on horseback. Down the spiraling stone streets and into the vast farmland. The men had ridden west toward Frostford, located on the coast. The trip would take a week's ride, but they were hoping to catch up with the King before then. They first rode through the Royal Plains. Passing windmills and fields of wheat and barley. Riding out of the basin, they entered the Dusk Hills, a region that stretched through most of the Highland realm, south of the Red Mountains. These soft hills were covered in dense pine forests. One would never find any plant creatures or Ones of the Wood here, though these western forests were no less wild. Bears and trolls roamed the mountainsides. The Dusk Hills were filled with old forts and villages. Much more populous than the Avarwood to the East.

The four knights rode past several of these small villages, asking town guards and citizens if they had seen any nobles that had come over from Castle Rock. They searched the coach roads and trails, but to no luck. No one could recall anyone notable passing though. Nothing apart from the usual traveling merchants. They rode further to a citadel, Fort Redmont. It was a town walled with stone, but nothing impressive. It once served as an army outpost in the days of old. Now, shop keepers and commoners made use of the abandoned military buildings. It was near dark by the time they arrived, but the inside of the walls were well lit with torches and fires. Going under the portcullis, the knights entered quickly looked around the courtyard. Igran went ahead and galloped his horse around the perimeter.

"Damn," He muttered. He looked frantically for any sign of the King's passing but found nothing.

"The horses need rest, Igran," Adir suggested. "We've worn them tired, if we do not stop-"

"No, we need to keep searching," Igran trotted his horse around again and then turned it about, inspecting the scene. "Damn."

"The King won't be under any stones, Igran. Give it a rest, we can stay a night and leave before dawn tomorrow, continue for Frostford," Ragnar said. Igran shot them a look of disapproval. "We are going to find a place to lay our heads for the night. Feel free to join us when it suits you best," Ragnar and his brother both rode to a nearby tavern. Delwyn pulled the reigns and brought his horse next to Igran.

"Aye, I may not be very wise," Delwyn prompted him. "But I have also been driven mad with determination. Any duty, any petty crime in my village, and I would cease at nothing until the job was complete. The others... Well, the others would laugh at how lawful I was. They'd tell me that I needed to relax and not take my duties so seriously,"

Igran rested his tense shoulders and was drawn into what Delwyn had been saying. "Hell, one of the knights from my village convinced me that a troll was spotted nearby. I stayed watch for several days, until I found out he had tricked me. I know this is more important, but-"

"I understand what you're getting at. Perhaps we both are so stubborn with our responsibilities, that we become unaware to what is practical. I let my guard down once and I paid for it. I just don't want to fail our King," Igran said then turned his horse toward the stables. "Now, let's go find where those bastards ran off to, probably best to check wherever serves the most mead."

Igran and Delwyn hitched their horses at the stables and walked to the tavern known as the Red Barrel. It was a stuffy place, wood furnishings and cast-iron utensils. There was a bard near the fire playing a lute that was just barely heard over the sounds of everyone's conversations. A mug of ale seemed to be the only drink on the menu and, for the most part, everyone was content with that. Ragnar and Adir were at a table in the center of the tavern. Both men were laughing at their own stories of when they grew up in the North.

"There I was, face to face with the Beheader, most feared creature in the Northern Reaches!"

"Grow up Ragnar! We both know you've never seen *the* Beheader. No one has ever encountered that giant and lived."

"Did, too! I came across him while hunting near the lake. The blade of his axe was the size of a dog sled and the handle was as tall as a pine. No telling how tall the giant himself was. He swung at me, but the ice beneath his feet caused him to slip. The beast was so heavy, he crashed through the ice and sank into the lake. Just enough for me to grab my kill and run. *That* is how I survived and don't you forget it!"

"Convenient no one else was hunting with you."

"I never said I killed the giant, just survived it."

"Are we interrupting?" Igran asked.

"Not at all. Come, sit," Ragnar welcomed the two other knights as they sat down at the table. Adir shook his head at his younger brother's story. "I see you have found our lovely establishment," Ragnar lifted his mug.

"We are here to rest, not to drink," Igran suggested as he moved the mug further away from Ragnar.

"One in the same to us," Adir paused as he was in the middle of taking a drink of his own ale. Igran looked around the inn. Many were simply enjoying conversations or getting lost in their stein. Two men in hooded cloaks sat in the corner, they locked eyes with Igran as he scanned the room.

"Come on, let's go," Igran said and turned to leave. The men followed Igran over to the haybales surrounding the stables. "This will have to do for tonight," They sat on the ground against the wooden stalls, holding their weapons and shields close. None of them minded the smell or scene of horse stables. For Igran and Delwyn, it reminded them of growing up as page boys, assisting other knights in their respective stables during their years of training.

Morning came and Igran was the first to wake. He heard the sounds of horses leaving the pens. He looked out and saw the two cloaked men from the night before riding out of town. Igran quickly mounted his horse and went out to follow. He rode out to the trail, which was misty in the cold of morning. Echoes of footsteps could be heard from the mist. The knight continued forward until he realized the sound was moving towards him. A dark mass appeared from deep within the fog. The footsteps rang louder with the clashing of steel. Igran pulled his horse out of the road and into the forest. He took watch from behind the trees as a company of soldiers marched out of the fog. They wore splint mail armor with purple sashes. They were coming from the West and continued past the fort. Lines of men all marched in unison. They didn't turn to notice Igran, but rather kept their bearing forward. Their sights clearly set on their destination. After their passing, Igran rode hard back to Fort Redmont.

"Get up!" He ordered as he arrived back at the stables. He had come in so fast; he did not notice that the men were already up and preparing their horses. "Come on! There was a whole company of men marching on the road."

"What in the hell are you talking about?" Ragnar questioned.

"Aye, a whole company. Now come on!" The other knights mounted their horses as they rode steadily to an overpass. They caught a glimpse of the soldiers as they marched into the mist. Several of the men carried banners that were made of the same violet shade that the soldiers wore on their armor. The banners were pristine and had a black crow in the center, who had a ribbon in its talons that read 'Power and Might.'

"What is this?" Adir turned to Igran for answers, who also shook his head in disbelief. "That was at least two hundred men."

"I have never seen an army like this before. I do not recognize the coat of arms, no lord that I know of bears it," Igran uttered. "We should get back to the keep, inform the local guards. See if they have any knowledge about this."

He turned his steed back and headed for the old fort. The others were soon to follow. They rode up to the portcullis to where they found several guards on overwatch.

"Fetch your captain immediately! Go, it is of much urgency!" Igran commanded the guards, who were aware of the knights' authority and obeyed his command without hesitation.

"Captain Ballard, sir!" The guardsman bolted into the barracks. "The King's knights wished to see you at once."

"Very well," He got up from his desk, where he had been examining some parchments. Meeting the knights in the town square, he was thrown off by their edge. "I assume you all have dire news for me, otherwise I wouldn't have been disturbed."

Delwyn called to him from atop his horse.

"A whole company of soldiers marched down the road this very morning, none we have ever seen or heard of before. Would you happen to know who they are or who their lord is?" Ballard shrugged. "Sir, do you know who they are?"

"I would guess they are just some nearby guards parading around. It is no cause to make a scene of."

Igran had a scowl on his face, his eyes piercing Captain Ballard. The captain looking around impatiently.

"Now, Sir Delwyn is going to ask you one more time," Igran said, grabbing onto the hilt of his sword.

"Who are those men?" Delwyn asked sternly. Ballard let out his anger through the exhale of his nose.

"I was sworn not to say anything. For the sake of my town and myself, I mustn't."

"I assure you, if you tell us it will work out better for you in the end," Ragnar pitched in, also making known of the warhammer he was holding. Ballard only looked down at the dirt and shook his head.

"As you wish. We are done here," Igran kicked his horse. "Coward," Him and his fellow men circled around Ballard, then trotted out of the town and turned down to the path that led further westward.

Back in Castle Rock, Sir Ulfer had fallen asleep in his chair and being of old age, slept for a long while. He woke at the sight of two guards putting a cover over his head. They beat him. The old man cried out in excruciating pain.

"Ack! Somebody..." A blow to the back of his head knocked him unconscious. The two men dragged him by the shoulders down the spiral staircase. Princess Evangeline and her brother Ivan woke at the sound of the commotion. Each of them came out of their rooms, to only see the empty stool where they had last seen Sir Ulfer. Evangeline ran down the stairs, with her brother close behind. As she turned the corner, she was captured by Grev, who grabbed her forcefully at the bicep. For his weak appearance, Grev held her thin body with an iron grip.

"Just the princess I wanted to see," He smirked. He hadn't noticed Ivan, who at this point shoved the old man off of his older sister. Grev returned to backhand the prince. "That is no way to treat your elders, son!" He snapped at Ivan. The prince reached for his hip but realized he did not have his sword on him. Guards came from behind Grev and seized both of the siblings. Ivan struggled to release himself but was met with a blow to the abdomen. He coughed in pain.

"Now, let me explain something to you," Grev began, "In the event that the King should… *disappear,* a regent is set in his place until he returns. And alas, as we can see," The old man gestured to the empty throne, "There is no King. So, until your father decides to stop being a mouse, *I* am king."

"No!" Evangeline vocalized. "My brother is heir to the throne, he should be placed as King, not you!"

"Your brother is a boy! Now you best listen here. Anyone who does not wish to believe in the way of our kingdom is to be considered a traitor," Grev walked to the throne, then turned to the corner of the hall, to where Ulfer was shackled to the stone brick. "And will be tried as such," He sat down on the King's throne, taking in the feeling of its power.

"Tis funny," The princess said. "It looks a little big for you," Grev's smirk died quickly and his face trembled with rage. He struggled to control his newfound temper.

"Lock them up in the dungeon," He muttered sternly to his guards. They promptly took the two away to the lower corridors of the castle. "This kingdom will soon see my reign."

Later in the evening, a guard in a black cloak pushed open the castle doors. He rushed to the King's throne. Grev stood near the fireplace along the wall, drinking a glass of wine. He stared intently into the fire as he thought to himself.

"What is it?" The old man asked, annoyed that his peace was interrupted.

"Gabel has escaped. We were ambushed near Crossroads and he ran off to the woods."

"He..." Grev hissed, looking to make sure no one had heard the guard. "He escaped? We have to act hastily now," He whispered.

"Yes, sir. We tried-" The guard was grabbed at the throat.

"The only reason you are not dead right now, is so you can find him. Get some scouts and get moving," The old man released his grip. "I will have Gabel dead. Do you understand me?"

The guard rubbed his throat for relief and then fled. Grev went to his seat, a wooden stool by the fire. He sat, glaring at the grand throne. Fire reflecting off his eyes showed the rage burning in his heart. He took a swig of wine to finish his glass.

Three brown horses took off from the city, their riders in black cloaks and hoods. Heading west toward the coast, they traveled much quicker than the caravan of guards that took the King. Reaching the road sign, the three halted.

"This is where we were ambushed," The one guard told the others. "Barris, Bosa, you go west. I'll go to the north. Search for him quickly and discreetly. It'll be all of our necks if he don't find him."

"Power and Might, Davis," Bosa said as a farewell.

The two whipped the reigns on their horses and took off toward Crossroads. Davis turned to go north. Riding with great speed, he made his way up the mountain base and across the valley of Three Mile March. Over the far mountain base, this rider saw a large village. Farms filled the bowl of land to the North of the mountain range. Steeples and windmills stuck out above the lush fruit trees and fields of wheat.

Weaving along the switchbacks, Davis walked his horse slowly into the City of the Prophets and dismounted it in order to search on foot. The hooded guard meandered through the market streets, bustling with farmers and clerics. He scanned the bright crowds as well as the shadowed alleys. Many wore simple clothes or priest's robes. None resembling the likeness of a High King. Davis turned to make sure he wasn't in anyone's focus before slipping into a back alley. Turning a corner, he came to a back door of one of the pubs. The guard pounded on the wooden door a few times and waited. The door was opened and standing in the frame was a heavy cook wearing an apron.

"What is it?" He looked around to make sure he wasn't seen talking to the cloaked guard.

"Send out men to look for the King. He may have escaped here," The guard said quickly in a soft voice.

"He *is* here. One of our scouts saw him enter the city. He's staying at the monastery. Do you want us to go after him?"

"No," The cloaked guard refuted, careful to keep his voice down. "Not yet. I will ride back to the garrison in the mountains. We'll take the city. When we come, have your men ready to attack the monastery and kill him."

"Alright," The cook looked both ways down the alley again before closing the door and disappearing back into the pub.

The Apprentice

Myles, get on the billows! This fire needs more heat," A bristled man called as he thrusted a steel blade in the forge. A lean young man ran to the other side of the outdoor forge. He had on an apron over simple clothes. His hands and face were covered in soot and sweat. His copper hair was tied back in a bun.

"There it is, keep the air coming!" The older blacksmith ordered as Myles pumped the fan. Taking the glowing red blade out of the furnace, the blacksmith dropped it on the anvil and swung down with his hammer. The superheated steel sparked as it was shaped. He turned it over and struck the other side, molding the blade further. The ting of the hammer against steel rang out into the town square. It was morning yet, so the market stalls were not nearly as crowded as they would be at midday. Horses pulled carriages and riders through the dirt streets.

Crossroads was a trading hub from the western coasts to Castle Rock. All the paths a farmer could take inland fed into this town. The great road going West of the capital also intersected with a trail towards the North. Despite the frequent travelers and merchants, Crossroads remained small in population. The hamlet nearly had more inns than town homes.

A hiss of steam formed when the sword was plunged into a wooden bucket. Taking the sword out of the water, the old smith wicked off the droplets and set it on a table on top of a pile of similar swords. Myles took a rag and wiped his face as he stepped up to the table.

"Been quite a while since we've had a large order of weapons," Myles said. Then took one in his hand and lightly swung it around.

"It's not a sword yet, only a blade. And a rough one at that," The old smith chuckled. He rubbed his bristly beard as he observed the pile. "Yes, quite a while... Some lord wanting to arm his personal guards or whatever."

"I didn't think there were any keeps out this way. Saint George has their own smith and so does Redmont if I remember."

"I don't know, kid. I just take the gold and make the steel. I wouldn't think on it too much. Besides, you can't sharpen all these swords if you're lost in thought. Now get on it," The old smith loosed his apron and threw it on top of his other tools. Myles dropped his sword arm and brought the weapon over to the grinding wheel. Pumping his foot on the wooden pedal, the stone wheel started to turn. Once it picked up speed, Myles held the edge of the blade down to stone. It sparked and crackled. The apprentice moved the blade up and down, sharpening the whole edge. The blade had a diamond-shaped cross section, so all four faces had to be sharpened.

Myles went through the whole stack of blades. Each taking careful time to sharpen. The master smith worked to polish the blades, filing the rough metal down to smooth, shining steel. After the blades were finished, the smith took them back to the furnace to finish assembling the hilt. Myles jumped back to the billows and fanned the flames. The tangs, the rods that stuck out from the blade, were put back into the forge.

"Get the cross piece," The smith said to Myles. The young man went around to the workbench and grabbed all the pieces that would make up the hilt. Pulling the blade out of the furnace, the smith held it towards Myles. The apprentice slid on the steel crossguard, then the grip, and lastly the pommel, a large round piece at the end of the grip. The tang protruded passed the pommel, just enough to be hammed down and secure the hilt in place.

"Nice work, son," The smith set the blade aside. "Now just a few dozen more."

"Could you deliver these for me?" The smith loaded the wooden crates of swords into a small horse drawn wagon the next day. "I'd make the trip myself, but there's work to be done here yet. Mister Tidings needs me to repair his shop sign."

"Sure," Myles said and took off his apron and climbed onto the wagon.

"Thanks, lad. Shouldn't be too far, the men who ordered these said they're camped between here and Saint George."

Myles whipped the reigns, and the horse took her first steps forward. Its hooves clicked on the ground as it pulled the carriage out of the town. The hills were covered by large pine trees, shading the road below. Needles from the pines littered the red dirt and kept the grass short in this stretch of woods. Several merchants passed by on the road, which was paved in cobble near the towns, but otherwise was simply a line of packed dirt.

"Morning," One merchant waved from the top of a cart loaded with goods from all over the realms. Ingredients and elixirs, tools and trinkets, craftsmanship and the like came from the West. Whereas the Royal Plains produced crops, milk, and wool which would be sent out to the coastlands.

Myles drove the cart until he smelled a roast over a fire. Looking ahead, he saw a city of tents and men in splint mail armor sitting around. They wore purple sashes and undershirts. The camp had crates scattered around with bird cages next to them. Myles at first suspected hawks for sending mail, but the cages held large crows. They cawed over the quiet woods to alert the men of his presence. Pulling back on the reigns, Myles' horse slowed to a stop. He peered to see if they would give any indication that these were the men in the woods he was supposed to meet. It wasn't uncommon for wayfarers or crooks to camp outside of towns. But a camp this large was uncommon.

"Hey!" One man barked. "What are you looking at?"

"I'm here to make a delivery from the blacksmith. Was told to bring it to a camp in these woods," Myles said from the wagon.

"Yeah," Another soldier stood from his seat by the fire. He was tall with a scarred complexion on his face. "We ordered the swords. Bring 'em down," Officer Harlow was his name. His hair was black and cut short. His face was kept roughly shaven with a knife.

Myles stepped out of the cart and went round back to grab one of the wooden crates. The young apprentice struggled as he carried the heavy box over to their camp. The men chuckled at him in amusement. The scarred soldier drew one of the swords and let it hang in his hand. He gripped the hilt a few times then swung it about.

"A decent enough blade."

"Finished and sharpened just yesterday," Myles said.

"Were they now? Yes, they still have that fine shine. Not quite scuffed up yet. Though, that's just a matter of time, isn't it?" A few of the soldiers laughed. "What do you say, lad, ever stained one of your blades?"

"Never had the need," Myles said.

"Lucky boy. You should carry one with you. Dangerous world, this is. You'll never know when you'll need one," Harlow swung at Myles. The teen jumped back. The other soldiers laughed, Harlow snickering as he lowered his sword. "Give him the gold for the swords," The scarred soldier ordered. Another got up and went to fetch a bag of coins from the tent. "And an extra piece for being a good lad," Harlow patted Myles on the back as he handed off the gold. The other soldiers returning to their business. The apprentice sighed with relief. He climbed up into the wagon, got the horse to turn around, and rode off.

"Officer," One of the soldiers said to Harlow. "Just received word. Ballard's ready for us to occupy the fort."

"Very generous of him to have agreed to our terms," Harlow replied. "We'll pack up and move in day after tomorrow."

"Yessir."

The Attack

Two cloaked riders slowed their steads when they reached the village of Crossroads. The riders walked their horses along the village streets, not minding the folk walking beneath them. The markets were bustling, stall vendors were busy selling their harvest or baked goods. Inns and pubs had a constant flow of patrons. One pulled back on the reigns of his horse when he saw three men in an alleyway. Two were taking boxes out of a wagon and showing them to the third person. The riders were about to move on when he saw the men present a gold crown with silver decorations. The other showed a greatsword that was glistening with light.

"Barris," The rider said simply. He turned his attention down the alley to also see the exchange. "Ride ahead to the camp. Tell them the King's hiding here."

"Very well. Power and might, brother," Barris kicked his horse to a trot. Once the townsfolk started moving out of his way, he picked up speed and rushed out of town. Bosa softly turned his horse away and continued to blend in with the town's crowded business.

Barris galloped into the pines to a city of tents. Canvas hung between the tall trees and was pitched into the red dirt. Men were busy packing crates and tearing down their shelters. Dismounting his horse, he walked into the head war tent.

"Once the battalions finish their rounds, we should be ready to march to Redmont," An officer with scarring on his face said to the other officers in the tent. "If Grev hasn't secured the capital from the inside, then we'll send a detachment that way."

"Officer Harlow," Barris walked in.

"Gabel was supposed to be delivered here days ago. What happened?" He accused.

"The caravan was ambushed, and Gabel escaped. Grev sent me and a few others to search for him. Yet we believe he is in Crossroads."

"What makes you so certain?" The officer asked.

"We have seen the King's Sword and his crown there."

"If that is true, it will be hard to find him in such a populous village," Harlow thought.

"If he hasn't already ridden back to Castle Rock," Another officer said.

"He knows it's not safe. He'd be a fool to return," Harlow shook his head.

"We could launch an assault," Another officer put in. "We are at that stage in our plot. If Grev is on the throne, then we can begin scorching the loyalists."

"Very well. We'll send a company to launch an attack. The rest of us will make for Fort Redmont," Harlow nodded. He turned back to Barris. "Go back to Crossroads and inform our sympathizers of incoming attack. Ask the villagers who their King is. Teach them the reason of their demise."

"Yes sir. Oh, and… the King's knights are close at hand. Grev sent them this way."

"Yes. They were spotted near Redmont. We'll show them our forces soon enough."

Barris bowed slightly then turned to leave. He walked back to his horse, grabbing a bird cage on his way. Barris held the cage in his lap as he kicked his horse to move once again. Behind him, he heard bells ringing to order the soldiers to prepare for a battle. Barris smiled to himself, knowing the few guards stationed in Crossroads would not be prepared for a surprise attack.

As Barris shortly arrived back to the crowded streets of the village, he opened the bird cage and released a handful of crows into the air. They cawed and perched themselves on the tops of buildings and on signposts, scaring off the smaller birds. Bosa and the other sympathizers saw the crows and moved to evacuate from the village. Crossroads was far too crowded and frequented to notice a half dozen men leaving in a hurry.

"People," Barris asked loud enough to make himself know in the market. "Who is your King?"

"High King Gabel," One woman stood up. Others nodded along with her.

"Then you have put your faith in the wrong man!" Barris announced and then rode quickly out of the village. The folk in the market looked to each other in confusion, most just returning to their business. A merchant was unloading sacks off potatoes off of a wagon and onto the ground. As he reached to move another bag, he saw there was an arrow stuck into it. The older man looked behind him to see a hailstorm of arrows falling into the village. He scrambled to flee as arrows pinned down villagers behind him and cut through the canvas coverings of wagons and stalls. Soon not just arrows rained down but fire as well. The flash lit up the markets and roared as the fire grabbed onto the wooden structures.

Stationed guards rung the bell tower, but it was too late. The soldiers in purple were already storming the outer village. Foot soldiers advanced after the barrage from the archers. They ran with spears and swords, jabbing anyone trying to flee. A hooded man on a wagon whipped his horse to run away, but a fireball blew his wheel apart. He and his goods were thrown from the high wagon. As he crawled towards his valuables, a soldier stepped on his back and brought his spear straight down through his spine. The soldier ran to find another victim to strike down, without noticing a bright sword that lay near him.

"Get out of here!" A bristled man yelled.

Myles, his young apprentice, ran out of the smith shop. Fire burned around him as he was being chased down by soldiers in purple. They sliced at him, but the nimble young man dodged. He dove through the wall of fire to escape their blades. Landing on the ground, he saw a weapon that shown like silver in the burning grass next to him. He picked up the sword and swung to ward off his oncoming attackers. His copper hair came undone and fell in his face as he rose. The soldiers surrounding him paid no fear to the young man having a weapon. Yet as one charged, he side stepped and cut across, slicing the soldier's neck. More attackers came at him, but Myles countered skillfully. He parried and deflected; no soldier able to cut his skin. He raised his eyebrows, amused at his natural talent.

"Myles, get out of here!" His master called to him, who was defending himself with his forging hammer and a sword. "Run!" The young man didn't lose grip of his sword as he turned and ran into the forest beyond the village.

Meanwhile, the royal knights were making way towards Frostford. The road was winding through the pine forest, climbing up into the mountainous regions.

"Do you smell that?" Adir asked the other men. "It smells of burning," The other men nodded and looked about for the source of this scent. "There, smoke!" Adir pointed above the treetops to a pillar of smoke that was rising from within the forest.

"Ya!" Igran whipped the reins on his horse and bolted to where the smoke was originating from. Delwyn and the brothers not far behind. The men weaved their horses through the trees. Dirt flew as the stallions booked it across the land. As they drew near, screams could be heard, and the sight of flame become more present. Soldiers, wearing the same uniforms as they had seen before, were burning the village, and slaughtering the townsfolk that lived there. The knights took up their weapons as they charged into the burning city of Crossroads. They knew these men had nothing but evil intentions.

Delwyn had his shield at the ready as he ran down some of the attackers. The soldiers on the ground were still cutting people down with their spears. They turned to the knights who charged them through the flames. One raised his spear, to pierce the horse that was coming at him, but dropped it in fear. He turned to run from his attacker. Igran, who was chasing him, came up with his sword and cut at the man's spine. He fell in agony, only to be trampled by Igran's horse as well.

The brothers dismounted their horses and advanced on several soldiers who were attempting to kill off several more villagers. One lunged forward with his spear at Adir, who stepped away but was still sliced at the side. The cut went through his chainmail and slit a little into the flesh. Adir, who wielded a war axe, hacked at his foe. He missed the first blow but came on at the soldier's neck for the second. The soldier screamed but was soon silenced by another slash of his axe.

A blast of fire hit Ragnar in the back. The warrior turned to see a mage preparing another fireball. Ragnar raised his shield and ran toward his enemy. It was a large round one that was painted into four sectors. The two sectors on the sides were painted green with a charging ram facing the steal boss in the middle. The mage threw what fire he had at Ragnar. It dispersed over his shield in a cloud of smoke but didn't slow the knight down at all. From behind his large shield, Ragnar brought up his warhammer and broke the mage's jaw. The cloaked enemy fell back on the ground. He reached for his own face, hoping to heal himself, but Ragnar swung his hammer down and crushed the man's chest.

Nearby, Sir Delwyn drove his horse to one of the soldiers. He was flanked by another, who came down on Delwyn's left. The attack was blocked by his shield and the knight turned to cut at the soldier with his sword. The other man, who Delwyn was first pursued, jabbed his spear into the horse's torso. The animal let out a terrible cry at is flailed to the ground. Delwyn's leg was still caught underneath its body. He sliced at a soldier's shin, warding him off. The soldier raised his spear, readying himself to stab down at Delwyn. But the attacker's head met the end of Ragnar's warhammer. The soldier collapsed instantly, Delwyn could see the crater that was left in the man's helmet. Ragnar pulled Delwyn out from under the horse and brought him to his feet. They both braced quickly as several more soldiers drove blades in their direction. A spearhead glanced off Delwyn's shield but was redirected to his calf. The knight quickly countered the attack and brought his sword across his opposers chest.

Igran kept two hands on his greatsword as he dueled with the soldiers on the ground. He attacked with rhythm, swinging his sword to the right and left of his enemy. He blocked with equal precision, walking backwards to defend himself. Igran lunged at the soldier, who took another step back. Tripping over a fallen beam, the soldier was struck down as he fell. Igran quickly turned to find the next enemy. He saw a town guard fending off two purple soldiers. Igran ran to aid him when he heard screams coming from one of the buildings set ablaze. He changed course in an instant and hurdled into the burning shop. Through the smoke he saw a mother and her children trapped behind part of the upper floor that had collapsed.

"I'm going to get you out of here!" He shouted over the roar of the fire.

"Take my babies!" The mother cried, holding out the toddler. Igran grabbed her and then reached for the other, older child. He paused for a moment to think about what to do. The mother waved him away, coughing in the thick smoke. Igran ran out of the building and set the two children down behind a stack of crates.

"You stay hidden. Understand?" He ordered. "Adir! Lend me your axe!" He yelled as he dove back into the building.

"Dammit," Adir said under his breath as he ran to follow Igran into the fire. Adir chopped up the debris with his axe as Igran kicked and threw other burning pieces out of the way. The woman was on the ground in the corner, gasping for air. Once there was enough cleared, Igran rushed in and picked her up. The two knights charged out of the shop as it soon collapsed behind them.

Adir was then blindsided by a soldier, his axe flying out of his hand. He quickly returned blows, punching the soldier with his metal gauntlets. They tackled each other to the ground. They rolled through dirt until the soldier ended up on top. He wailed on Adir, eventually getting his hands around his neck. The soldier choked Adir and held him down as the knight struggled to get free. Sir Igran came from the side and kicked the soldier in the chin. He collapsed onto the ground and was hastily stabbed by Igran's sword.

The battle slowly settled, the royal knights taking out the remaining soldiers with the town guards. They went around the remains of the village and aided those who survived the massacre. They pulled folks out from under the wreckage of their shops. Their clothes were now charred and tattered. Their skin was dirty and, for the most part, burned as well.

"Thank you, kind sirs," A woman wept as Delwyn helped her to her feet.

"Why did they do this?" Delwyn softly asked the woman, who was clinging onto him for support and comfort.

"They came..." She muttered, trying to conjure words through her tears. "They came and asked us who our King was," She gasped as she spoke to him. "We t-told them that it was King Gabel. He has been our King for so long, I thought it odd for them to ask," She began to cry again.

"Then what happened?" Delwyn kept her going. She took a couple deep breaths before continuing on.

"Then they attacked us, called us 'faithless'," She sank down to the ground and began to weep.

"I don't understand," Delwyn turned to Igran.

"Nor do I, not entirely," He replied. "But I am willing to bet this is all connected. The King disappearing, a new army rising under our noses. God, I wish I knew what was going on back at the castle... See if you can find a horse that's unclaimed. We have to keep moving. Adir!" He called across the ruins. "Stop collecting weapons, we're moving out!"

"Aye," Came echoing from behind the forge. Igran shook his head, then looked up to the woods. He saw a man in black hiding behind the trees.

"You there!" Igran called out. The man realized he had been spotted and began to run for the woods. Delwyn started to leap after him, but his calf was still wounded and gave out.

"Blast!" He uttered to himself. Ragnar, however made his way to catch up with the man. A loud 'ow' was heard just moments later. Delwyn and the others looked up in anticipation.

"Got 'em!" Ragnar's boast came from within the woods. Igran helped Delwyn to his feet and they proceeded to where Ragnar was. As they came around the brush, Ragnar could be seen pinning the man against a tree. This man happened to be a lot smaller in size than his adversary. He wore a black mask over his eyes and a hood on top that. The man brushed away Ragnar's grip, knowing it was no use to resist these men.

"Who are you?" Igran asked of him.

"If I said, you will most certainly throw me away," He replied. "I'm a highwayman. Rob people who pass along the roads. Rich folk."

"Then we have no use for you," Igran grumbled.

"Wait," Delwyn interrupted. "Have you robbed any noblemen within the last couple days? Any one of a particularly high standing?" Igran raised his brow at the question.

"Depends, was the man you were looking for dead or alive?" The crook joked. Ragnar shoved the thief back against the tree. "I might have had a recent heist. My gang was robbing this small parade of soldiers, much like the ones you met in town," He gestured towards the burning ruins behind them. "They were carrying many dead nobles. One however was still alive, but while we were trying to 'free him of his guards,' he may have slipped away…"

"But this man survived? What did he look like?" Adir asked.

"Oh, yes he was very much alive. He was older, very fancy attire though. Red cloak and furs. He was in good shape for his age, I'll give him that. He took off with my horse. Ran into the woods, but we didn't bother to chase him."

"Anything else?" Ragnar pushed him further against the bark of the tree.

"We figured they were the King's nobles. We took from the heist a crown and a sword. That's all I know, I swear to it," The thief shook his head. The knight dropped his grip and before they could say another word.

"Go," Igran ordered. The crook scrambled to his feet and ran into the woods. Igran scanned the woods to see where the soldiers might have come from.

The Garrison

Beneath the once glistening Castle Rock, the prince and princess were locked up in adjacent cells. The dungeon was humid and dark. An odor of rats and insects came strong from several of the cells, which in previous days hadn't been used, so they were left empty for pests to move in.

"This is my fault," Ivan muttered as he hung his head. "I should have stopped him; I should have known!"

"No, Ivan. This is not your fault. That wicked man is to blame for this, not either of us. You know that father-" Evangeline stopped short as she heard the sound of the cellar door being unlocked. Grev came down the steps, with Ulfer close behind. Ulfer's body was covered in burns and blood, he wouldn't dare look up. The princess gasped as she saw her loyal friend had been so brutally beaten.

"What have you done?!" She clung to the cell bars.

"I taught discipline to those who had none. He was a servant of the King, as he is now. It is now time for you to make a similar choice, my dear. Unlock the cell," He turned to Ulfer. His hands shook in chains as he took out the keyring. The trembling key had a hard time finding the lock, but eventually the old knight got it. As Grev entered the small cell, Evangeline sank back into the corner. "You have nothing to fear, my dear girl. You just need to bow and swear your life to me, and you will not be harmed."

"What?" She wore a terrified expression.

"Just listen to him," Ivan piped in from across the iron bars. "Just listen to him and this will all be over."

"Yes, listen to your brother. This is your last chance. I am being crowned tomorrow. Your father is gone but you can still save yourselves if you serve me," Grev held out his crooked hand for her to kiss his ring. Evangeline stepped forward. She approached him, only close enough to reach out and slap the elder man across the face.

"You will never be a King," She said.

"You hag! Guards bring this witch out to the courtyard!" Several armed guards with purple sashes came in and apprehended the princess. She kicked and protested, and they struck her multiple times. "We shall show the people of this kingdom what happens to traitors."

The soldiers dragged the princess out of the cellar and into the main hall. Grev immediately behind.

Ulfer looked over to Ivan, the young prince remained silent. The old knight sighed then proceeded up the stairs. Blood dripped from Evangeline and stained the red carpet a deeper shade. They jerked her around as they brought her toward the double doors, trying to restrict her as she ceaselessly fought. The doors were pulled open and the princess was thrown down the steps into the empty courtyard. The ground was cold in the fall morning.

Leaves blew around from the garden. The city on the other side of the greying walls lay silent. The red banners fell to the sides of their towers in the light wind. Evangeline crawled to distance herself from Grev as he rushed down the stairs.

"You may not believe me as your king, but that does not change the facts that your father is *dead*, and I am on the throne. As any ruler knows, their kingdom can only be strong if their followers are loyal. And you, my dear, are the essence of disloyalty. To keep you alive would only spread your false ideas."

"No," The princess got to her feet and continued to back up as Grev walked toward her. "My father is alive."

"Lies! He has died. And with him, dies the age of oppression."

"My father did not oppress."

"No? What caused the years of rebellion? What caused an army to rise up against him? Unless… Maybe he was not such a great guy. The King oppressed my people by restricting our magic, banning our divine power. But the shackles are gone. The people of the West can be free," Grev reached out and closed his hand, in his fist formed the hilt of a sword. The fiery blade came into existence as he pulled the blade closer to himself. From the top of the stairs, Ulfer gasped in horror. The two guards also looked on with shock.

"By God, what is this?" Evangeline shook.

"This is our liberation," Grev raised his flaming sword.

"No!" Ulfer hollered. The old knight grabbed the sword out of the sheath of one of the guards and charged into the courtyard. His hands still shackled together. Grev lowered his arm and turned to his opponent. The two old men standing a few paces apart.

"Are you betraying me, old man?" Grev's eyes were fierce as he readied his blade.

"I am knight of the King. I was never yours to betray," Ulfer, with tears in his eyes, readied his own sword. It shook in his old hands, but his grip was firm.

"You dare…" Grev lurched forward and swung down with his sword. Ulfer deflected the attack, then sliced across at his foe. The blades clanged as each man exchanged attacks. Sparks fell from the flaming blade as it chopped and sweeped. Each old man took his time between attacks, the other careful to block. The sounds of steel echoed in the empty garden. Ulfer grunted as he lunged his sword forward, Grev side stepped and struck the old knight's back. He cried out and tensed his muscles as he turned back to face Grev. The regent grinned and readied his flaming sword. Ulfer raised his and lunged again. Grev cut across and sliced his wrist, the sword falling onto the stone ground. Before Ulfer could arm himself again, Grev's sword was thrusted through his gut. The old knight, exhausted, looked down at the blade that pierced him.

"No!" Evangeline covered her mouth. Ulfer then closed his eyes and fell onto the ground. Grev dispelled his sword and stared down at Ulfer's body.

"Lock her up in her quarters. She doesn't leave that tower," He hollered. The old man not taking his gaze from the knight. The princess was in too much distress to fight the guards that came. They grabbed her by the arms and dragged her back inside. "This one has paid for her."

"Sir, the King was not found," A messenger stood before Harlow, staring at the ground. The officer was standing behind a desk in the barracks of Fort Redmont.

"Blast," He spat. "Anything else?"

"The King's knights showed up and cleared the rest of our company. Only a handful managed to escape." Harlow glared at him, breathing heavily through his nose. "Should I send word to Grev?"

"No," Harlow snapped. "We have this under control. Word's been sent that the King might be north. We won't show up light-handed again. If he's there, we will crush him."

"Yes sir," The messenger nodded. "And the knights?"

"We cannot take the time to send men out to find them. Our focus has to be the King. Though perhaps someone else could hunt them down," Harlow moved to get his quill and ink. He scribbled onto a piece of parchment as he spoke. "Send this off to Lord Bramus in Frostford. Tell him Grev has a special use for his... particular talents."

"Right away, sir."

The messenger took the letter, rolled it up, and put it into a cylinder container. He stashed it in his satchel with other letters and notes to be delivered. He bowed and left the barracks, walking out into the town. Soldiers filled the old fort, ordering the citizens around and having their fill of the pubs. A few soldiers were even cornering women in the alleyways. The messenger passed all of this as he mounted his horse and took off, away from the garrison and toward the West.

As more of Grev's soldiers moved into the area, they began to camp in groups outside of the fort. Soldiers sat around fires at night, dotting the dark forest.

"Can't believe we have to wait in the woods while our officers are enjoying feasts already in the fort."

"You heard Harlow; not enough room inside for the reinforcements."

"And what's the delay? Ballard opened the fort to us. Poor choice to leave your army out in the cold, I'd say."

"It's not even that cold, quit your whining," The soldier picked at the venison roasting over their campfire. A handful of soldiers sat on the ground or on logs with him. All of them eating and drinking from waterskins.

"So, what's the news in the capital?" One spoke up.

"Grev's been turning over the guards. He's putting the ones from the West in charge. Most of the old ones have been responding to the change of administration, though. Grev supposedly took care of the ones still loyal to Gabel."

"What of his promise to us? Will the old man honor that when the war is done?" Another asked. "I can't wait to be done sleeping in tents."

"Looks that way. Lot of folk are moving out of the city. So, there'll be plenty of room for us to move in."

"Who're the refugees now?" He laughed. "Soon enough we'll have a home again."

"And the heirs? I know he got Gabel out of the way, but what's being done about the prince and princess?"

"They're both being kept in separate cells, last I heard."

"What do you mean?"

"Grev wants them convinced the other is dead to deter them from rebelling against him. Told each of em the other had been executed," The soldiers around the fire chuckled. Their laughter stopped when they heard a branch snap outside their camp. A young man with copper hair stood dead in his tracks.

"The hell is this?" A soldier got up to his feet.

"Sorry, I was lost," Myles began to back up.

"Yeah, you are," One soldier drew his sword. "Get over here!" The soldiers charged Myles, who took off running through the deep woods.

"Where you going?" They called after him. "We only want to talk!" But Myles had outran them and was gone from their sights.

The Paladins

North in Sanctuary, Ezemiah was preparing the King for his return journey. The sun had just risen, igniting the autumn leaves in the valley. The other monks were gathered in the temple, praying and singing. Ezemiah and the King were in the stables, readying a horse.

"Will you really return to Castle Rock?"

"It's what I must do. If Grev has taken the throne by disposing me, then it shall be an easy retrieval."

"I do not think you will go unopposed. If Grev has forces in the mountain, surely he has supporters elsewhere."

"And do not I?"

"I did not say that. But there are hard times ahead, my King. Do you still not trust in my wisdom?"

"My friend, your wisdom is as far as your beard. I trust you," He paused. "You're just not very encouraging."

"You know that's not my job," The old prophet said. "All I can do is speak the truth."

Singing rang out from the temple's open windows. Monks in white and brown robes davened an old hymn.

A story passed down from generations, with each telling it was seen as more fable than fact. Yet these monks recited the tale with reverence. No number of years — which they had plenty of — would make them forget. They would always remember what the world around them had long forgot. They sang:

God came from high
And walked his earth below, the earth below
He formed a King
And gave him life with snow
God led this King o'er all the ground
And there from earth, his people found

He pulled the dwarves from stone
And elves he found in wood, deep in the woods
In fires and ash, the great orcs stood
And men, he dug from dirt
He faced all creatures of the earth

There was no place God hath not walked
No beast in fields unstalked, no beats unstalked
God left with the sun to the West
His King would soon be laid to rest

But now we're left in lives of strife
To toil against the night
To sing the songs of old, sing songs of old
To not leave his name untold

Gabel stood in silence. He fixated on the hymn, the old creation story of a King who pulls each race of the kingdom from the earth. Dwarves from stone, elves from wood, orcs from ash, and man from dirt. A King who roamed over the whole earth and faced the great beasts of old. A King who walked with God. A King whose lineage was passed down to Gabel.

"Now hear the truth. The God who walked with Greyland, walks with you, my King," Ezemiah spoke softly. "Find your strength now and do no lose it."

"Adonai guard you, friend," Gabel tightened down the saddle and stepped on the stirrup to mount his horse. Ezemiah went across the dirt courtyard to open the gate. A large crow cawed from the walls of the monastery. Other crows flew above the town and perched on rooftops.

"They are here," The prophet turned sharply. Soon screams came from the village as farmers and priests rushed behind the town walls. The marching of soldiers could be heard from the South. Splint mail armor noisily gave away their powerful presence.

Gabel drove his horse uphill into the vineyard to see the size of the invasion. From the mound with the lone tree, he saw a hundred soldiers flooding from the mountain into the simple village. The King turned his horse around and rode back down to Ezemiah.

"Have you any defense? Any guards? Anything?"

"The Fervent knights are too few to hold off this army. They are the only ones in this city to hold a weapon,"

Ezemiah stroked his beard in stressful fear. "I wouldn't suspect pitchforks would hold against these men."

"There must be something here! Or will you send your King to battle without a sword?" Gabel asked his old friend as he got down from his horse.

"There is *one*," Ezemiah quickly led the King into the back entrance of the stone temple. "Brothers secure the walls," He ordered the other monks who were still in prayer. Taking a torch from the stone wall, the two descended down a set of stairs into the lower sanctums of the monastery temple. The basement had several rooms off from the main chamber. In a chamber off to itself, lit by a smoldering torch, was a stone table. On it, lay a large weapon concealed in cloth wrappings. Ezemiah went straight for this table.

"What is that?" Gabel asked from across the room as Ezemiah went to unwrap it.

"It is the sword of Gath, whom you killed in these mountains," The prophet lifted the cloth.

"I swung it once in battle, that is a sword of giants," The bronze craft shone dully, still in perfect shape and sharpness.

"Do I lie to you now? You are Gabel the Strong, High King of the Realms. Take it, you will find no finer weapon."

Gabel breathed out slowly as he picked up the greatsword. Holding it in two hands, he held in vertically in front of him, realizing he possessed the strength to wield it. The bronze reflected his own image, a King without his crown.

"Go. Call your knights. We'll ride out the side gate."

"Sire?" Ezemiah questioned.

"The army's here for me. If they see me leaving, they may yet spare this place. You said the Fervent would aid their God, now go," Gabel spoke with authority and at once, Ezemiah left. Going up the stone stairs, the old prophet went into the sanctuary of the temple. The monks now taking shelter and praying as the soldiers began to siege against the monastery gates. The wooden palisades could only take so much.

"Ring the bell, brother Akiel," Ezemiah ordered, interrupting the monk's prayer. Yet at once, the robed figure got up and went for the bell tower at the front of the temple. Heaving down on the fraying rope, the heavy iron bell began to ring out over the whole village. It was a low ring that was distinct over any other.

Across the town, an old grey-haired farmer in white gambeson heard the alarm. Putting a cloak of white on over that, he belted his sword around his waist. Securing leather bracers to his wrists, he then drew his sword before running out of the house. As he ran from the fields towards the town, he saw other knights in white cloaks running in from the outskirts.

"You can't go!" A woman called to a young man as he pulled on his cloak. "Edwards, don't go out there."

"Mother, I must. I swore an oath," The man pushed out of the farmhouse and sprinted into the smoking town. Soldiers overturned the streets, burning the wooden structures and chasing villagers down with spears. Edwards drew his sword as he joined the fight.

He checked one as he ran by. He slashed and elbowed, not slowing his run. Knights in white pushed through the storming soldiers, cutting them down with their swords. Fighting their way to the monastery, the knights slowly gathered as a more unified group.

"Open the gate!" Edwards yelled. Monks on the other side of the wooden palisade lifted the bar and allowed the five white knights to rush in. Immediately, the doors were pushed shut and barred once more.

"Ezemiah, what's going on?" The older knight asked, still catching his breath.

"Brothers, this army is after the King."

"So why attack us?" Edwards spoke up.

"Because the King is among you," Gabel declared as he mounted his horse, the bronze sword on his back.

"Are we King's men now?" The old knight turned back to Ezemiah. "We are holy warriors, the Fervent don't take orders from royalty."

"Gabel is fighting on the side of Adonai. And so, do you!" Ezemiah shouted over the roar of battle behind them. "I will not argue with you, you must escort the King out of here!"

"And leave our families behind?" The older knight challenged.

"Cedric, do as I say!" Ezemiah snapped. "You were to already be detached from this world. The Fervent fight for one cause, and that alone! Do not forget that your King is from the line of Greyland, the King who walked with your God."

Cedric scoffed as he and the others went to the set of horses already prepared for them.

"Never in my life have I heard such a thing," Cedric said as he mounted his horse.

"Knights this is your duty. You take the King to the refuge. You listen to him!" Ezemiah ordered.

The wooden gates were now being pushed apart and weakened by the army fighting against it. Fire burned up part of the monastery wall, smoke filled the whole village. The Fervent knights looked back at this, hearing the slaughter.

"Go now! These men will lead you to Castle Unknown," Ezemiah shouted to the King as he ran ahead to open the side gate.

"The capital, Ezemiah."

"No. It is not safe. Now Go!" Gabel took off without another word, the knights in white following behind. The army outside the village now diverted their attention to the fleeing King. The few calvary they had sprinted to cut them off, but they could not catch the knights. Inside Sanctuary, the monastery walls were busted in and hordes of soldiers in purple sashes flooded the holy place. Not paying attention to the onslaught behind him, Ezemiah began to say a blessing over the King, now ridden out of sight.

"Do not fight for yourself, but the one who is to come. Have faith in what you will not see until the setting sun. May Adonai be with you as he is with me. Always walk in the light and so may it be."

As soon as the prophet ended the verse, he turned back to see his monastery in flames. The soldiers now falling back from the village, returning to the mountains, leaving the village to burn down in their wake.

Gabel was long gone at this time, driving hard across the land. He only slowed when he realized the Fervent were not keeping up with him. Turning back, he saw one young knight that had stop a ways back, still looking in the direction of the rising smoke. Gabel trotted his horse up to Edwards.

"We must keep moving."

"I left my family back there."

"Son, we must go."

"My family died because of you!" Edwards turned and shouted. His brown curly hair, dripping with sweat. "They couldn't even defend themselves. You Kings and your wars, this is all it brings! We vowed to fight for what is holy!"

"Do not blame me for the men who attacked!" The King's raised voiced silenced the young knight. "I do not wage this war. I don't go out of my way to conquer villages or level them, like *they* have! You heard your prophet; you are your God's Fervent. His fighters, yet you cower at the idea of battle. Do not think I have no idea what it's like. My children are in the castle with the monster who launched this attack. Everyone in these Realms are my people. I feel the weight of their lives, too. I do not wage war, but war is at hand. Brace yourself like a man, sir knight. War is here."

Gabel turned his horse around whipped it to continue riding over the hills. The knights turned to follow, eventually Edwards did as well. Riding out of the rolling plains, they found themselves entering the forested East.

The Lord

Saint George was a rather large village. It lay on a gentle summit in the Dusk Hills, well above the pines. Frost was beginning to form in the ground and the wind blew cold across the hilltops. Above the rest of the town, a great stone temple reached above the summits. Yet no one remembered the name of the God it belonged to.

The knights riding into the town's epicenter appeared as a strange sight to the simple folk in the village. Their armor was scratched and dirty. The men had bandages over their battle wounds and dried blood on their weapons. The knights hitched their horses and made way for the town's mead hall. The innkeeper covered his nose as they entered and pointed toward the bathhouse across the square.

"You men are welcome to stay as long as ya don't bring yer stench in here with ya," The innkeeper said. The knights then rolled their eyes as they left out the door.

"One ale," Ragnar said over his shoulder. "That's all we ask for."

The knights went over to where the bathhouse was, drew water, and dumped it over themselves. The grime on the men's faces came off, and so apparently did their smell. After they all were done refreshing, they went back the mead hall. The innkeeper seemed a bit too satisfied that the men were now clean.

"Please my fellows, do come in!" He opened the door for the knights, who simply acknowledged the man rather than converse with him. They went straight for the bunk house, sprawled out on the bedding, and slept till the next dawn.

The knights of their King rose that morning and broke fast. The innkeeper providing bread and cooked eggs. The brothers, Ragnar and Adir, went out into town to seek the head of this village. Whom, at this age, was a lord by the name of Sven. He was found in the guildhall, which sat on the crest of a hill, down from the village.

"I caught wind of the royal knights coming into town," Sven welcomed as the brothers approached. He had long blonde hair which was tied back. He wore a fancy brown doublet and had a sword at his hip. "Oh, it eases my heart to see with thine own eyes, such men of chivalry. Come," The baron walked the knights to a room where other higher-class folk congregated. "I am wondering what I can do for you. Alas, I have heard the grave news that the King of the Realms has gone missing."

"Afraid so," Adir assured the lord. "We were sent out to find his majesty but have a dead trail."

"Have you then heard? A new king has been crowned in his absence."

"Ivan?" Ragnar asked.

Lord Sven shook his head.

"Well then who in the hell is left to take the throne?"

"I have not heard of this nobleman, he calls himself Grev," Sven answered. The two knights looked at each other. "My courier came by and recalled that they had been sentencing citizens to death. Anyone still loyal to King Gabel was done away with. Yet you both look as if you know this man or at least not surprised by the news."

"Aye," Ragnar said through the clench of his teeth. "He's the bastard who told us to set out for the King. I ought to have beaten that man when I had the chance."

"Grev tricked us to leave the castle," Adir started, "But we had no choice. His men had abducted the King, we knew he didn't run off," Sven nodded at this, taking in what had been told to him.

"Grev's men have not come after Saint George, fortunately. Yet, news has been brought by my men, that he is forcing the hand of the other lords to join his side and swear their loyalty to him. The Realm of the West obviously is on his side. Silverlands, maybe... No ruler has done this in all the history of these lands..." Sven explained. Ragnar shook his head and went to stare out the window.

"Aye be of some cheer. Saint George and his men owe their allegiance to King Gabel, the true King of the throne. We will aid you in whatever task your kin may need. We have good horses and strong men, all of which are at your bidding," Sven told them.

"Much appreciated," Adir said.

"And please, make yourselves home here. I'll cover whatever that innkeeper charges you."

"The King thanks you," He bowed slightly.

"Not as much as you will. The feasts here are excellent. Please, help yourselves," Sven waved for a servant to pour them wine. They sat down on the large oakwood table. Ragnar allowed himself to smile when he saw all the food set before him.

Igran and Delwyn were still in the mead hall, talking to the local villagers and tradesmen. They asked the knights wearing their gallant armor, why they had traveled so far from Castle Rock to come into a hamlet like Saint George.

"We were driven out into the wilds in search of the King," Who the folk of the Realms at this time knew was missing. "Anything helps us to find him if you know of anything."

"Did you hear of the attack?" One old man blurted.

"We were at the attack," Igran said. "Crossroads has been destroyed."

"Not Crossroads. Another one. Just the yesterday an army in purple marched on the City of the Prophets and leveled the whole place."

"What?" Delwyn asked, shocked.

"The Army of the West," Igran concluded. "I don't know if it would be worthwhile to investigate another ruined village."

"The Army of the West? The old rebels?" One of the bar's patrons looked up.

"Aye, I'm afraid they're back and with much larger numbers than before," Igran answered. The townsfolk sat somberly at the thought.

"Did you find anything?" Adir asked as the four met up later in the bunkroom of the mead hall. They sat around a table that was lit by a few candles.

"Another town was sacked. Sanctuary, to the North," Igran sighed. "Hope you have better news for us."

"Not so," Ragnar said. "Grev set himself as regent. So, it's confirmed he's behind this all."

"Damn," Igran huffed. "What of the prince and princess?" Adir shook his head softly before replying.

"Grev's been killing people in the city if they don't vow themselves to him. Just like the villages. I'm fearful to think what's become of them."

"Where did he get the men to pull a takeover like this? How long was Grev planning to do this?" Delwyn asked.

"My guess, since their defeat in the Red Mountains. But where he got the men this time, I have no idea," Igran sat back in his seat, exhausted. "Very few westerners survived the uprising. The remnants were the old or sick, but that was twenty-some years ago. It's very likely these are the sons of rebels. Grown up knowing the King was responsible for their family's deaths."

"It's not looking good for us," Adir shook his head. "We've been fooled to leave the castle and now we're outmatched in our own kingdom. If he has his grip on our army…"

"Look, we can't stop Grev's campaign and there's nothing we can do now about Castle Rock," Delwyn spoke again. "But we have a lead to the King. That's our secret weapon now. If we don't know where he is, likely Grev doesn't either."

"We can't go trampling through the mountains. It's a day ride to Sanctuary, at least. I say we recruit. See who's still loyal and get them ready to fight!" Ragnar protested.

Delwyn was about to refute when Igran raised his hand for them to stop.

"No, you're right, Ragnar. We can't all go looking," Igran said. "Delwyn and I will ride out to Sanctuary. You two stay here. Get this town armed and ready."

"Saint George is loyal; the lord here supports us and will spare his men."

"Good. Ride out to neighboring villages. Rally men here. You'll have to march East and take Redmont once you have the men."

"We'll do what we can. Let no man stop you," Adir said. "For the King," He lifted his mug.

"For the King," Delwyn nodded. Just then Sven walked into the mead hall, waving to the innkeeper and others in the room. There was a fire crackling in the large hearth, heating the whole building from the cool air outside.

"It is my honor to be of service to you all," Sven greeted the knights.

"Afraid Sir Delwyn and I must be off already," Igran said in passing.

"Where are you going?" He asked.

"We have reason to believe the King may have been in Sanctuary. We have to find him," Delwyn answered.

"I see. I can offer you some guides for your journey. The mountains can be hard to traverse."

"Delwyn, let's go," Igran called form the door.

"That would be appreciated," Sir Delwyn turned back to Sven.

"Talk to the men working the stables, they'll ride with you," Sven patted Delwyn on the back as he left. Sven then went up to the front of the mead hall, standing with his back to the fire.

"People of Saint George, hear my words," The normally bustling hall grew quiet as their ruler began to speak. "We are entering an age of war; the tide is rapidly approaching. If we do not stand firm, we will be swept away. The throne of the true King has been taken, usurped by a filthy traitor. Now, this ruler of falsehoods has begun to drive the Realm into fear. Pillaging each village that not bows to his feet! Alas, he has another thing coming. Doth he know of Saint George and his people?" The men inside grew excited at the call, fire raged in their hearts and the blaze could be seen through the eyes. More men came in and filled the hall to hear the commotion.

"We must stand together, not only as the people of this village or this region, but as one Realm! We must rise up from the wake of his destruction. Stand with unyielding loyalty to the real King. But we need men, fighters, great warriors in order to ever wish to restore the throne. I call upon you, any able body to take up the sword. The Realm of the King needs his army, and it reaches out to us. The King reaches out to *you*. Grab your swords, your bows, any weapon you can carry. Hear this! Saint George must take up this fight. Now what say you? Will you raise up your weapon in defense for your kingdom, as I? As these brave knights have?"

Sven seem to be on a pedestal, the words flowed from his soul as a roaring river. A young man in the chorus gave out a proud "Aye!" Then another man stood and spoke the same. Then another and another. Soon every man in mead hall, practically every man in Saint George, pledged their allegiance to this newfound army. Goblets were raised, and a great chant began which shook the earth in its power, "Long live the King! Long live the King!" It was loud enough to stop Delwyn and Igran in their tracks as they began to ride out of town.

Down the slopes and across the plains of the kingdom, Prince Ivan sat silently in his frozen prison cell. His black doublet was torn ripped and covered in dirt. The moisture in the air began to freeze onto the cast iron bars in the cool of the season. Light stretched its comfort faintly from a lone torch at the head of the dungeon. Grev opened the door leading into the dark place, it clanged against the stone walls. His crooked stature took up the small frame of the doorway. On his head was a crown of silver with amethyst stones.

"How is royalty treating you now?" Grev mocked the prince who was broken in spirit and curled up on the floor. His weak breath could be seen, but he had no words for his captor.

"I have a use of you," Grev continued, "I am in need of a squire in my court. It's not as glorious as your past position, I'm sure. But it's better than spending your last days in this cell wondering what will kill you first, starvation or the cold. You wouldn't want to die like your sister, now would you?"

The young man shook his head. Ivan was brought out of the dungeon and into the throne room. He was made to stand to the right of Grev, who sat in his father's throne.

For weeks, Grev's army began to fill the city. They stood like statues on their posts, guarding Grev and his supporters. They wore helmets that covered their faces and purple sashes over their splint mail armor. Bands of soldiers searched throughout the city and brought forth anyone who spoke out against Grev or anyone who claimed Gabel as King. He had these commoners brought into the throne room for inquisition; his soldiers threw one of them down before Grev's feet.

"Do you know why you are here?" Grev asked the man, who trembled in fear. "You plebeians have no respect for true, divine, authority. You live in denial, in belief that your wretched King is still alive. Gabel abandoned you at the first sight of danger and now he is certainly dead."

"Divine?" The man looked up and asked. "The King's line was established by God. *His* rule was divine. You kings set yourselves on thrones because you are not placed there by God."

Grev turned to his audience, a mixture of his loyalists and those also waiting trial.

"Allow this to be a lesson in case my previous demonstrations haven't made it clear enough. A kingdom cannot run if traitors like this clot the flow of things. Perhaps I shall remind you all that I was the one noble who stayed to look after this kingdom, while those others wealthy bastards took off and ran to their deaths. *I* was faithful to this Realm, when not even your King was!" The crooked ruler then stood from his chair and went over to the man who did not lift his face off the stone floor.

"Ivan," Grev said.

"Yes, your highness?" Ivan replied.

"Kill this man."

"What?" The teen looked at the peasant.

"Kill him. Or will you be a coward like your father?" Ivan stood and did nothing. "Very well."

Grev held out his wrinkled palm over the commoner. Ivan was astonished to see that Grev's hovering hand was crushing the man, but by no natural force. It was a trick of sorcery that gripped the man, the curse tightened its grip, contorting him. Grev, with a sick smirk, raised his palm softly. The peasant was lifted by the magic and held suspended in the air. As his invisible hold tightened further, the very bones of this man began to crack under the pressure. Then, a swift fire leaked from Grev's hands. The flames made passes through the man, scorching even his insides. He attempted to cry for mercy, but the pain of his collapsing chest made him unable to do so. Trails of fire went in and out of the peasant. His shaking stopped abruptly, as his body now hung lifeless. Grev dispersed his magic and the peasant's body fell hard on the stone, breaking whatever bones that were still intact. Grev cleared his throat and stepped over him.

"I beg you, my people… Do not end up finding his fate. I shall shed my mercy on you this once. Go now and serve your true king. The power I wield shall prove as a guarantee of my authority," The rest of the towns people were escorted out by Grev's soldiers. He then turned to Ivan, looking for a response.

"I was unaware you had these abilities," Ivan, still nearly speechless gave Grev the reply he desired.

"Ah, you were unaware… I did much greater things than these. Much greater things. My magic was suppressed by your father. He claimed only certain magic practices were ethical in the kingdom, the 'Noble Magics' they were called. Healing and petty spells were all it would allow. But I was brought up by a different breed. I studied a fiercer, more powerful style, the one your father banned. The Western Magics. My order perfected the most powerful spells, rivaling any that had come before us. Your father must have felt threatened by my powers, and perhaps rightly so. Powers unseen, unheard of. Powers of fire. That power is what a true ruler should wield."

Grev's old muscles were weary after performing such spells. He slouched in the throne, blankly staring off at the warm corpse, whose blood found the creases in the stone panels.

"Wouldn't you say I have the power to rule?" He asked the son of Gabel.

"Yes," Ivan said. "Truly."

"Yes… Dispose of him," Grev muttered to Ivan and pointed loosely at the body. The prince cleared the lump in his throat and went to drag the body away. His garments, which were torn, and dirt covered anyway, now had a fresh stain of blood. Grev then waved some of his guards over. "Take the princess down to the dungeon. Neither can know the other is alive," He whispered.

"Yes, my king."

The Troll

North of Saint George, Sir Delwyn and Igran, along with two villagers named Lochlan and Fergus, rode through a desolate mountain pass. They made their way to a trail which wove up the rocky slopes. The horses made easy way up the tracks. Along the trail, springs and simple creeks transcended into spectacular falls. Water fell like a vertical river, plunging into the wilderness below. As they entered the Red Mountains, the land became dense with pines again. The peaks nearly cutting through the blanket of trees.

Dusk soon came upon the men, which forced them to break for camp in a small valley. This hidden pocket rested between two peaks of the same mountain like a little biome, stowed away from the rest of the world.

Lochlan and Fergus were sent out to gather firewood as Delwyn hitched the horses to a large tree nearby. The two villagers bantered back and forth between the trees, looking for dead wood to collect. Igran cleared out a place for the group to lay their bedrolls, kicking away pine needles and rocks.

Once the wood was collected, Fergus rapidly rubbed one of the sticks against a larger log. It began to darken and smoke, and eventually the splinters in the log caught flame. Smaller twigs and needles were gently placed on the flame and the fire began to breath and mature. It slowly overtook the larger sticks and became bright and hot. Fergus set another log on top of the teepee then sat back to watch his fire sustain itself.

Soon, the men began to talk and share stories. Legends that seemed only on the edge of what could possible. Lochlan told the story of Sir Conner the Copper. He was a knight who was blinded by a dragon that spat acid in his eyes. This knight then, while stumbling blindly, knocked over a pile of rocks which set into motion an avalanche that in turn, killed this dragon. The knight knew no one would believe his tale, so he single-handedly dragged the dragon back to his village. All the way from Wyvern Hole to Frostford.

Delwyn told a tale from the Avarwood. That one night a mage was wandering through the woods and started a fire to keep himself warm. The fire consumed a tree that was held sacred by the Ones of the Wood. They found this mage and imprisoned him by growing into a large tree around him. The mage had nothing to eat except the moss off their bark. The plants grew year after year until his body was fully grafted into their trunks. His very blood feeding the trees.

"Twas an old tale they told children to keep from starting forest fires," The knight added. The men were fascinated by each other's campfire stories. They laughed at others larger than life fables, but eventually calmed into silence.

"To be honest, I am nervous for Sven," Fergus spoke up. "Not that supporting the King isn't a good cause, but he is eager for redemption and I don't know whether or not that will blind his decisions."

"Do tell," Igran looked up.

"Sven's father, the late Lord Johan, brought disaster to Saint George. Out in the quarry, one of the miners struck gold, enough to support our villages for years to come. Johan decided to build a temple in praise for this fortune. He took every mason and sawyer the town had to construct the building. At first, it seemed good, an honorable thing to do with the resources we had. But it pulled all of the men out of their fields and into one location. Saint George was sacked by vikings from the North, all the women and children in the outer villages were slain and the men didn't even know.

"Johan took his men to war against the pillagers. It was a long-fought battle, many men died that winter, and the great Saint George was left empty and lord Johan was left with no one to rule and the biggest temple in all the Realm. Eventually, people moved into the open farms and repopulated the city. Sven is weighed with the task of rebuilding what his father lost. The people all know the story and watch Sven's every move. So, I hope and pray that when he goes to battle, he doesn't pull out all of his men, leaving the town vulnerable. We want to support the cause, but we also need to think of our homeland."

"Best we can do now is hope," Lochlan said and laid down to sleep. The others soon joining.

A terrible roar came out and woke the men. Horses shrieked and kicked at their post. The men scrambled to their feet and saw a large shadow against the pale dawn light. A troll. The size of six men it was, ugly and fat, trying to pull one of the horses away from its reins. The beast let out a roar from its huge gut. The rope snapped as the troll lifted its prey above its terrible jaws. It had tusks like a boar, cracked and yellow. It held the horse with one hand, a crudely built axe in the other. The handle was a tree snapped in half and the blade was a large piece of slate rock, broken off from the mountain.

The troll was met by several strikes to the shin by the knight's steel-made weapons. It dropped its meal, the horse kicking up to its feet soon after and darting off into the vale. The behemoth kicked the men off its shin, which was wrapped in simple fabrics like most of its clothing. It lifted its axe and swung downward with great force, bellowing as it did so. It dented the earth with the blow but missing any target.

The troll staggered to pick up the rugged axe for another strike. Delwyn charged the fiend, with one hand firmly on the hilt of his mighty sword, the other holding his shield. He cut up into the beast's side, the blade piercing between the ribs. It hollowed and swung down at him. Delwyn jumped to get away, rolling down a steep hill. His sword and shield flying out of his hands.

Fergus scrambled to his bow and quiver. He distanced himself from the troll as he fired. The arrow sank into the back of its neck. The troll sharply turned locked eyes with Fergus. It roared and started to chase him down. He slung the quiver over his shoulder and ran between the trees. He turned back to fire another arrow, this one lodging into the troll's thigh. It was slow as it tried to follow the man through the dense pines. Eventually, Fergus stopped when he realized he was no longer being followed. He caught his breath and nocked another arrow, peering through the forest to find his foe. The pines before him were chopped down with a single swing of the troll's axe.

"Help!" Fergus yelled as he ran away again. The troll, chopping down trees as it followed him. Lochlan pulled out his spear, still packed on the horses saddle and ran towards the fight. Once he got sight of the troll, Lochlan threw the spear into the back of its shoulder. It turned to face him, the handle of the spear snapping on the trees behind it.

"Shit," Lochlan realized he'd thrown his only weapon. He darted to the side as the troll now followed him. He ran to the hillside, jumping and sliding down the loose dirt. The troll took bounding strides down the hill to chase its prey. Delwyn was pushing himself off the ground when he saw Lochlan run by. His eyes nearly jumped out of his head when he saw the troll running towards them. As the beast charged by, he was kicked and thrown back to the ground.

It paused to decide which of the two men to go after. From behind, Igran jumped off the hill and drove his sword into the creature's back. The troll let out a cry of agony. It flung its great weapon around, cutting into the trees. Igran was thrown off by the motion. Delwyn saw his sword sticking out of the grass nearby. He crawled to it and slashed upwards, cutting the troll's heel. It tripped and fell backwards, taking a pine down with it.

As it was trying to lift its own weight off of the mountainous ground, Igran brought down his sword on the creature's chest. Its wretched smell was tainting the air. After a moment's struggle, the troll stopped breathing.

"Blast!" Fergus caught his breath from atop the hill. "Good work, men," The rest of them throwing down their weapons and taking a breather.

"Let me find that blasted horse," Lochlan said as he went back to their camp.

"Find it quickly. We need to keep moving," said Igran. His voice echoed in the dense forest. "Who knows what else sleeps in these woods."

After the horse was found, they made their way deeper into the vale. The forest was dark at this early hour, the sun still hidden behind the mountain peaks. The tops of the trees wove into a dense canopy. The deep brush made visibility low, yet there was a presence that drove along the trail. Eventually, the forest was so thick, they had to get off their horses and lead them on foot. On the forest floor, the men spotted what looked to be a road, it was however small. The thin cobble path couldn't hold one man by himself, let alone the horses.

"It looks like a gnome path," Delwyn said. "We'd find these all the time in the Avarwood."

"Shall we follow this, my liege?" Fergus called back to Igran and Delwyn. They walked closer to where this path was most present.

"It gives us a start," Igran nodded and lead his horse down the narrow path. Others soon to follow. The path weaved redundantly through the forest, even crossing little creeks, which to no one's surprise, tiny bridges were built over them. After a decent time meandering on the trail, they came to a clearing where a small cottage was built. The soft grass faded into gardens as they grew nearer to the building. Delwyn and his fellow knight dropped the reins off their horses and walked closer.

"Wait here," Igran said to the others. "It may be best if we do the talking, whatever the situation brings."

"Aye. Our tongues may not be as sharp," Fergus admitted.

"You call us though if you'll be needing a hand, yeah?" Lochlan added.

The knights proceeded toward the hatchway of the cottage. Although it was small, it was still sized enough for a man to fit through. The wooden door lead into a large room, that was decorated with trinkets and tokens from all parts of the Realm. Shelves and chests were plentiful, though it was peculiar to the men to see them all filled with papers. Scrolls and books stacked haphazardly on the shelving, with miscellaneous pieces of parchment scattered about, even on the floor.

Delwyn inspected one journal, which was filled only with sketches of landscapes and sceneries. He saw drawings of mountains and forests and even settlements. He flipped further, then froze on one of the many pages. It was a sketched layout of a village, with a single stone keep in the center and across the square was a statue of a great warrior. Simple market stalls surrounded the town square and humble little housings nestled inside the walls of the village. A stone keep sanding over them. It was a map of Thundertree. Delwyn placed the dusty book back where he had picked it up, he turned to find Igran studying a map of the Realms, which hung on the wall. Pots clanked against each other in the other room. Both men refocused their attention to the noise.

"Who's there?" Igran clutched the hilt of his sword.

"I surely mean you men no trouble," A hoarse voice came out from around the corner.

"Neither do we," Delwyn replied, looking to Igran who was still suspicious. An old creature stepped around the corner. Hovering above his hand was the flame of a candle. He was very short kind of person, only about half the height of a man and rather scrawny. Pointed ears and a long, crooked nose. He had white hair which added to his age. He wore a long, rough cap and a white shirt with a dark blue cloak.

"Might I ask, what are you?" said Delwyn.

"I am Otstyr. A Wayfarer."

"We are sorry to disturb you, sire. We'll be going," Igran turned and grabbed Delwyn by the arm. "Let us not meddle with magic creatures," He whispered.

"Going where?" The creature asked.

"Passing through these mountains to Sanctuary," Igran looked back.

"And what could you fighters ever need in such a peaceful town?" The elder looked up at the two men from his staff, which was taller than he was.

"What is it to you?" Igran asked the old creature.

"Igran, you heard him. He's a Wayfarer. This one could lead us," Delwyn said.

"After he curses us," Igran muttered.

"The King has gone missing, and we are searching for him. We have reason to believe he may have been in Sanctuary," Delwyn looked down to Otstyr.

"Ah yes. The King has been to that place many times."

"And you would know?" Igran asked.

"Of course. Like this knight has said. I know the entirety of the Realms. My feet know every rock. My eyes have beheld every place."

"I've heard your stories," Igran started. "Wayfarers grant passage to one destination then they vanish. Most people are escorted to their deaths, their pockets picked clean."

"Most… I was the map maker for King Gunder before Gabel. I spent many years in service to the throne. I made all the charts, walked the entirety of the kingdom. Mapped it all. I lead knights on many journeys and brought them back again," He said in his scratchy voice.

"If we find out where the King is, would you lead us?" Delwyn said to the Wayfarer.

"Yes…" The old creature thought. "I could lead you."

"If you abandon us or lead us astray, I will personally execute you," Igran warned. "Finding the King is of utmost urgence. I will not have time to deal with your magic antics."

"Understood," He bowed slightly and dispelled his candlelight.

"Lead on then."

The Wayfarer

The men left the cottage and mounted their horses. Otstyr walked in front of them through the mountains, guiding their horses down an invisible trail. They wove between trees and walked around brush. They stopped at springs to let the horses drink and quickly get food themselves. The whole journey, Igran never letting Otstyr out of his sight.

"He's here to help us," Delwyn said to him as they stood away from the group. He was eating a small loaf of bread in between sips of his canteen.

"He may say that. Forgive me if I am untrusting, but I intend to be a knight who lives to retirement. It's this whole magic business that threw our kingdom into this mess," Igran said. He stood, leaning back against the rockface.

"Magic itself isn't evil. You can't hate him for being born into it."

"I've met few who have the gift and use it for good. Power like that corrupts. And if Wayfarers are as powerful as the stories say, then there's enough cause for me not to trust him," Igran said.

"Once we find the King, he can go. Most likely, he'll be gone tomorrow when we get to Sanctuary."

"Let's hope so," Igran said as he started toward the group. "Mount up, men. We push on."

The day eventually grew dark, the sun hiding behind the mountains that surrounded them. The men were tired of riding and the horses were getting slow. Otstyr stopped on a ledge that overlooked a ravine below them, well above the tree line.

"We shall stay here for the night. Tomorrow, we will reach Sanctuary," He said.

"No. We need to keep moving," Igran said from the top of his horse. The others groaning at the thought

"Trust me when I say it is wiser to camp here than to lead your horses across the causeway at night."

"The causeway?" Delwyn asked.

"Angel's Road," Fergus said. The Wayfarer nodded.

"We must cross the most treacherous land bridge in these mountains if we wish to get to Sanctuary," Otstyr said.

"You're leading us through the 'most treacherous' part of the mountains?" Igran accused.

"Finding your King is of the 'most urgency,' is it not?" He replied in his usual calm, but rough sounding voice. "This is the fastest way. It would cost days if traveled down the mountain to Three Mile March and back up again."

"Fine. We leave first thing in the morning," Igran announced. The others relieved they could get off their horses and stretch.

"You would tell us if there were any trolls nearby, wouldn't you?" Fergus asked the Wayfarer.

"Oh, I don't think you want to know how close we are to some things…" He said then walked away.

They didn't bother to make a fire that night. The men simply tied up their horses and rolled out their mats in the clearing. Otstyr leaned back against a boulder and covered his eyes with his large red hat. Igran stared at him from across camp, but eventually gave up and turned over to sleep.

The next morning, they were up and on their horses before breakfast. The sun greeted them as they climbed the rocky path to the summit. The light caused the clouds around them to glow a soft gold. The wind blew across the exposed mountain tops, chilling the men in their simple clothes and metal armor. As they neared the top of the mountain, the saw a line of rocks that disappeared into the golden mist. The causeway was only three or four feet wide and dropped down hundreds of feet on either side. In the fog, they couldn't even see the ground below them. This thin stretch connected two peaks at the crux of the Red Mountains.

"Is it safe to ride on?" Lochlan asked.

"Better go on foot," Otstyr answered. The men got off their horses and stood before Angel's Road. The Wayfarer began walking out onto the rocky bridge. The men looked to one another to see who would go first. Delwyn stepped forward, his horse slow to follow. They spaced themselves out as they walked onto the misty causeway. The rocks beneath them were uneven and loose. The horses often slipped, having to keep track of all four feet. Rocks tumbled down the cliffside, often falling through the air for a hundred feet or more before they would hit the vertical cliff again and continue their fall. Other mountain peaks could be seen in the fog, sticking out from the clouds that passed through them. The wind kept on, pushing the men ever so toward the ledge.

They passed one particular spot where the rocks had broken away on either side of the causeway, leaving only a foot span. Delwyn and Igran were slow to cross, both having to pull their horses onward. Fergus stepped across and slipped. His grip tightened on the lead. As he dangled over the ledge, the horse's head was pulled down, causing the animal to slip. Its back hooves sliding off the other side of the bridge. The others were helpless to get to him. Fergus tried to pull himself up by the reins of his horse, but the bridle slipped off its head. He fell and grabbed onto a rock. His horse climbed back to solid ground, still shaking in fear.

"Fergus!" Lochlan yelled, trapped between the two horses. Fergus pulled himself up, but the rock started to loosen in its place. His feet scratched the side of the wall as he frantically tried to pull himself to safety. Eventually, he muscled his way back onto the bridge and laid on his back as he collected himself.

"I'm starting not to like this trip," He said. Igran glared up the causeway at Otstyr. The old creature looked back at the knight in silence, then turned to continue.

Soon, they got across Angel's Road and made it to the wide summit on the other side. Fergus calmed his horse down before mounting it again. All of them relieved to see such spacious ground beneath their feet. They rode off, downhill, and further North.

A trail came into existence as they grew closer to the edge of the mountain range. Flattened paths marked with cairns guided them around the side of the mountain and to the other side. Their path between the rocky tops eventually opened up. Great fields and forests lay now in front of them. The fields of golden hay and orange leaves. In the middle of the autumn colors was a scar of black that smoldered in the distance.

"Sanctuary…" Otstyr mourned.

"Do you have knowledge of all the land that has been burned? This is why the King must be found," Igran said as he kept his horse walking.

"Gabel was right to say one dragon was not an issue. Men do much worse," Delwyn added.

They rode on, making their way down the slope and into the farmlands. A few people worked the fields, taking off heads of wheat and storing them in baskets. All of them wore a numb expression on their face. The knights could easily see why. Their farmhouses were all that remained of this place.

The peaceful city of Sanctuary was now smoldering rubble. The remains of stone buildings stood out among the wooden ones that were burned to ash. Winding down the hill, their horses picked up speed. The smoke reaching up bleed into the overcast skies. As they rode into the ruins, monks were walking through the ash, collecting bodies, and looking for survivors to heal. One monk with a crooked walking stick walked out to meet them.

"Hail, knight," Ezemiah raised his hand to greet them.

"Hail. What happened?" Igran asked.

"The Army of the West."

"As we've thought," Igran scanned the ruins. "Did they have reason behind their attack?"

"We were holding someone they wanted, yes."

"Where is he now?" Igran pressed. Ezemiah looked at him for a moment and saw the royal crest on his armor.

"The King rode for Castle Unknown, to the East."

"I do not know where that is."

"You will not find it on any map. Its location is kept secret by my order. It's a stronghold in the forests east of Castle Rock."

"Thank you," Igran said. "Wayfarer, do you know of this place? Castle Unknown?"

"I have seen it before," The old creature said. Igran pointed east.

"Onward," He said.

"Godspeed, knights. Your King needs you," Ezemiah said before they rode off.

The Prince

Across the mountains, the town of Saint George was mustering his men. Farmers brought to the blacksmith their old tools to be refashioned into weapons. Wood workers and handymen were busy in their shops making kite shields and battle gear. Sven went to every home in the neighboring hills, asking for boys and men.

"Saint George is calling; will you answer him?" He asked of them. Many young lads came up from their farms and fields across the Highland Realm. The town breathed with men who had the desire to fight.

Adir and Ragnar stood on the ramparts on the wall of the village. They looked out to the hills and the forests below, the brothers could see over it all. They both had their eyes set to the East, where they knew their castle was.

"Do you think we will be enough, brother?" Ragnar asked. They both then looked to the company that was forming in the town.

"Aye, these men have good spirit. I have no doubt of that. Yet we only have maybe three hundred men, not nearly an impressive army. We only match one company of Grev's. And that's in numbers, not even in strength."

"Perhaps then, we should ride to the other villages and strongholds. Call aid of other lords, other nobles who have not fallen to Grev's reign. Muster more men to the siege. Sven takes pride in his people, you can see him now sparking fires in their hearts, but even he has to know this will not be enough."

"Agreed. We'll ride the lengths of the road in search of the few loyal men left. But mustn't we first wait for our King to return before our launch?" Adir asked.

"We may not have that luxury, as we gather our armies, surely our foe does the same. We may have to attack as soon as we're ready," The men looked down again at the crowds of new blooded soldiers. Men from all over the Highland Realm rolled in to join the fight. Ragnar sighed. "These men do not know the hardship that is waiting for them. The fire of war... It is relentless, ongoing misery."

"Ragnar, they will learn in time the grit of battle. They know the sacrifice they must take up, and they are willing. To die a warrior's death is honorable, especially when it is for your kingdom."

The next dawn came, and men were up to meet it. They pitched tents and made use of the old barracks. The recruits brought back to life the old fortress, repurposing it back to its intended function. The guildhall was set up to be the headquarters. Maps were laid out across the tables and the knights often met there with Sven to discuss strategy and intelligence.

Coming up the road was one young man. His copper hair hung down to his face. Stubble lined his pointed jaw. In his hands was a sword that shone like silver. He pushed off his legs as he climbed up the hill towards the village. Sven was in the town square meeting the recruits that came in. Most wore the same dirty clothes that this young man had on, but it was the sword that caught his eye. The other volunteers brought in old pitchforks or scythes. This was the first real weapon to pass through the town walls.

"Morning, traveler," Sven walked out to greet the young man. "Lord Sven, captain of this army."

"Myles. I've come to join your army."

"Come, let's get you some food. It looks like you could use it. Maybe some mead, too."

"Thank you," Myles said as he followed Sven to the mead hall near the center of the fort. Other soldiers were inside, filling their stomachs with food and drink.

"My village was sacked by knights in purple. Burned it to the ground. I ran into the woods and just tried to hold out and keep out of sight, but more soldiers are rallying near Redmont."

"How'd you hear of us then?"

"While I was camping in the woods, I saw quite the pilgrimage heading towards here. Men with tools and weapons. Overheard some folk on the road saying there was a resistance being formed."

"We're grateful you're here. Now, may I ask. Where did you come by such a blade?"

"I don't know. My village was on fire, the soldiers came after me. I just saw it through the flames, glowing white. It saved me, so I haven't dared to let go of it."

"Then you were destined for that weapon. Something divine gave it to you. Tell me, Myles, can you fight?"

"I can," The young man nodded. "I am also a smith."

"You truly are a miracle. Our smiths need all the help they can get. Now, go get yourself something to eat," Sven patted him on the back. Ragnar and Adir pushed open the hall doors and looked around for Sven. The lord waved to the knights and the two brothers made their way around the table to him. "Hail, knights. What do you have for me?"

"It is of our interest that we seek the help from other lords, they all have guards who are already well trained," Adir said.

"They may be trained, but they are guardsmen, not soldiers," Sven chuckled.

"Which is better than what we have. Most men out there do not know how to carry a sword. They are utterly untrained, and we are too occupied to be able to train them ourselves. We need all the men we can get, Sven. You cannot ask your people alone to take back the capital city and all enemies in between. We need to seek help from further villages, other lords."

"No," Sven sighed. "You're right. My love of homestead as perhaps gotten the better of me. Go, take whatever you need. Go and call forth more men."

"We will send them your way, dear friend."

With that, the brothers parted from the hall and packed their horses. Ragnar threw his shield over his back and brought with him his sword and hammer. Adir also packed an extra sword along with his war axe. They each packed food from the mead hall and filled wineskins for their journey. They went out to the road on their horses, taking off farther west. They travelled through the hills and highlands that were filled with villages and little farms. The road weaved over these gentle hills and in between patches of pine woods. The two brothers rode until they came across a farmstead just off the route. A band of women emerged from inside when they heard the horses.

"Sir knight!" One called out. The red-haired brothers halted their horses before them. They could see the women were carrying swords in their packs. This one wore an old suit of armor. Her long brown hair tied back.

"M'lady," Adir acknowledged. "What is it you all need?"

"We heard they are recruiting an army over in Saint George."

"Aye…" Ragnar assured hesitantly.

"We want to fight. The kingdom needs more fighters."

"I'm afraid not, dear ladies. Go home to your husbands," Adir denied them.

"Our husbands are dead. They were killed by those wicked men!" The men on their horses looked at one another. "We wish to take up the sword in their place, please good knights, we are strong and able as any man," One said.

Ragnar jumped off his mount and took out his blade from its sheath still tucked under the bags. He dropped his shield and approached the woman.

"Draw your sword," Ragnar called out.

"Brother..." Adir said from his horse. Yet the lady obeyed and drew her sword against Ragnar's. He slashed across at her, but she parried the attack with her own weapon. She jabbed at Ragnar, who simply stepped back and to the side. He struck her sword with his, but she returned the blow. The dance continued for a short time. The woman was angry with every action, Ragnar only grinning in return.

"I am impressed," He called to her. "You seem to know your way in a fight."

She landed several more attacks on his sword.

"Aye. She may be better than you Ragnar," Adir laughed.

"I fought for my homestead during the great rebellion along with my husband and my brothers," She struck another blow, more confident now. "I am Alessia. And do they call you Sir Lout?" Her female companions and Adir laughed at this remark. Ragnar paused, trying to process the insult.

"It means knuckle-dragger!" Adir called to his brother.

"Ah," Ragnar lowered his sword, taking in the slight reality of this statement. "Despite your attempt to guess my name, I am Sir Ragnar. The laughingstock on the horse is Sir Adir, my brother. Perhaps you have proved me wrong. You fight with more strength of than some men."

"Man or woman makes no difference. I am a warrior. Even my name means defender," The woman glanced then at her ladies in arms. "They too are capable as any; I beg you sire. I have passed your test, let us fight."

"Brother," Adir waved toward himself. Ragnar turned and walked to him.

"They're capable," Ragnar said quietly.

"They would not be accepted in Sven's ranks. Capable or not. We need to look elsewhere."

"You saw her fight," Ragnar pointed to Alessia.

"Ragnar... We must go on," Adir steered his horse back toward the road. Ragnar scooped his shield back up and climbed to mount his horse.

"Sorry m'ladies," Ragnar shook his head, then whipped the reins of his horse. Once we reached his brother, the two picked up speed and went further into the forest.

In the white city of Castle Rock, the streets were filling up with more soldiers than townsfolk. Old guards were easily persuaded to accept the new king and new soldiers poured in each day. Guards with purple sashes stood watch for any sort of disturbance. Those who did disturb the peace, as it was called, was met with the head of a spear. Guards also went about and confiscated all traces of King Gabel. Grev wanted to erase all memory of the existence of his rivaled ruler. Paintings of Gabel's lineage that hung in the great palace were also done away with.

Paintings on the ceiling were scraped away. The great pieces of art that hung from the walls were tossed into the street and burned. More often than not, guards would haul in a citizen even on the suspicion that they were still loyal to King Gabel.

Grev sat on his corrupted throne, steaming with rage at a man with a scar over his face. Officer Harlow.

"What do you mean Gabel never found?!" He stood and gripped the officer by the throat. "The task was simple, capture the old fool and bring him straight to his cell! How could that possibly go wrong?" Grev spat though his crooked teeth. Harlow clawed at Grev's hands to get a breath of air.

"I- I don't know," He gasped. "We scorched the towns he was hiding in."

"'I don't know…" Grev mocked the trembling man. "Perhaps it's in your best interest to find out!" Grev threw him to the floor.

"The King's disappearance hasn't hindered us yet. If I may-" The officer was wiped by a chain that Grev had conjured up with his sorcery. The false king lifted his hand for another strike of the chain, but his servant was already bleeding onto the floor.

"Gabel the Strong needs to be dead. I sense he is alive; I feel it. I can only truly be the ruler if he is gone forever. And what of this army forming behind our ranks to the West?"

"They're peasants, sire. Nothing more," Harlow put his hands over his face. "Our numbers are far greater than them."

"Make sure it doesn't become a problem."

"Yes, my king."

"Get up, you coward," Grev kicked the officer.

Grev had not noticed that Prince Ivan had witnessed these events. For he stood behind a pillar of the great hall, listening in on them. Ivan sunk back into the shadow and went up to his chamber, his hands shaking. His chest burned and his breathing was sharp. He couldn't contain the thought his father might still be alive.

Ivan paced around his room. He stopped when he noticed his wardrobe. Scrambling to find the key, he unlocked the wooden cabinet. Inside was the suit of armor his father had fashioned for him. The black steel was glittering with gold trim. The royal emblem, the crown with angel wings, etched in gold on the front of the breastplate. The young Prince stared at the suit for a moment before taking it off of its mannequin. He filled out the pieces of the fitted armor. He put his silver circlet on his head. He took the sword hanging from his mantle and held it with both hands.

"For the King," Ivan said to himself. He walked down the spiral stairs of the tower and entered into the throne room. In full armor, he appeared before his father's betrayer.

"How dare you?" Grev called over to him.

"How dare you sit in the throne of my father? He trusted you as his nobleman. And for a moment I had you justified, that you really were set in place while he was missing. But you were the one who sent him to his death!

Nay, but you didn't even succeed. My father is surely alive and well. He is where you could never find him, his reign will have no end!" Ivan took off his gauntlet and tossed it at Grev's feet, challenging him. "But you will. Now, I have thrown down my gauntlet, and as my father lives, I intend to avenge him for all you have done."

"You bastard! I shall strike you down like I will your father! As I have done with your sister," Ivan then pointed his sword at Grev.

"What have you done with Evangeline?"

"She resisted, as you saw. She fought against an army far too powerful and she paid that price in her bloodshed. She was slain for her resistance. Now you feel as though you could overtake me as well. You will surely meet the same fate. And I will have the pleasure of striking you down myself!"

Ivan lifted his longsword and brought it downward at his foe, still sitting in the throne, but was met with a blast of fire. Ivan staggered backwards in his heavy armor. Grev rose from his seat and started toward Ivan. Grev, the mage, wished into existence a sword of his own. It was long and sharp; the blade was white hot and set ablaze. Ivan looked at his enemy's weapon with horror.

He got off his knee and stuck a blow, which hit Grev's sword. Sparks of sorcery flew when the steel collided. Ivan attacked with fury, relentless strikes on his enemy, who in old age could barely keep up. Grev was in shock at Ivan's skill. The prince of the castle put a gash in Grev's sword arm. The elder man winced in pain. Ivan lowed his blade for a moment. Grev then close his eyes and the wound on his arm sealed itself shut.

"You fail to see my power; you are ignorant of who you are fighting!" Grev called out as he struck again, landing a blow to his enemy's armor. Ivan advanced toward Grev in return. Piercing Grev's cloaks with his blade, slicing another cut into him. Ivan lunged again, Grev sidestepped and brought the edge of his sword down on Ivan's back. The prince turned and swung to cut at Grev's face.

They clashed in the hall of the great Kings. Steel against steel, the swords glanced off each other in fury. Both drawing blood from the other. Sweat flew from Ivan's curly hair and dripped off his face. The hall was empty of servants and rang with only the sound of the metal. Embers flew from Grev's magical sword with every movement. Grev placed several strikes in a row to Ivan's torso. The burning sword charred Ivan's exposed skin and caused any cut to amplify in severity. The prince cried out in pain.

Grev, took his time between blows. The young fighter grew more careless with rage, his more experienced opponent kept calm and countered Ivan's attacks with ease. Grev parried and kicked the prince to the ground. He cut Ivan's leg between the plates of armor. The old man went to finish him, but Ivan blocked the swing with his own sword. Ivan swung at Grev's ankles and slashed through his heel. The old man fell back in excruciating pain. The old man couldn't focus enough to heal himself. Ivan took the opportunity to stagger to his feet and escape the castle.

Ivan was taken back at the sight of the garden. The burnt artwork of his heritage. The dead plants. He ran out of the court, from the backside of the castle. He staggered through alleyways to the royal stables. He ran through the back door and got himself to a horse. He heard the guards outside running the streets searching for him, their armor clanging with each step. The guards were halted in shock to see a horse bolt from the stables toward them. A knight fully armed riding on top. They tried to stop the horse, but the speed at which Ivan rode at them simply scared them out of the way.

The prince was able to snatch a spear from one of the fleeing guardsmen. He charged his way through the street, most people scrambling out of the way, only a few guards dared to try and stop him. All of which were trampled by the grey stallion or cut with the spear. The prince made haste out of the castle, he could hear guards calling for townspeople to stop him, but no one obeyed. The prince took off from Castle Rock. Fleeing through the farmlands of golden wheat. Past barns and fields and crops. Fleeing to the West.

Guards rushed to the great hall when they heard the regent yelling.

"Get a carriage," Grev grunted.

"Yes, sir," The guard ran out of the hall. Grev closed his eyes and held out his hands. The wounds on his ankles sealed themselves.

"Help me up, damn you," He snapped at the other guards. They pulled him up to his feet and escorted him to front doors. By the time the old man walked down the stairs and out the courtyard, a horse-drawn carriage was waiting for him. "To Farfair Hold. Quickly," He said as he entered the covered carriage.

"Yes, sir," The driver whipped the horse and took off.

The Battalion

Ragnar and Adir rode across to another village in the Dusk Hills. Haybales dotted the perimeter of the town. Straw also was packed into the dirty ground of the village. The wood buildings were small and close together. The knights did not know whether this tiny hamlet even had a name.

"The King calls for aid!" Ragnar announced. Those who were out along the streets didn't stop even to hear. "The King needs men to fight! Who will join?"

Soon the villagers outside went into their houses. Only chickens and a few dogs remained outside with the knights.

"Why won't they answer?" Ragnar asked his brother.

"I don't know," Adir looked around the remote town. On top of a neighboring hill was a small keep. From its tower flew a purple banner. "We should go."

"What?" Ragnar turned to his brother.

"This place has fallen. Come on," Adir kicked his horse and took off.

The two rode, heading back to the main road. They drove their horses further to another village. Again, the people sheltered themselves in their houses. None would answer the knight's call. Ragnar turned back to the road and went for another town.

"Wait," Adir called ahead to his brother. "Ragnar, wait!"

"What?" The knight pulled back on his horse.

"This hasn't been fruitful. We're not going to recruit anyone out here."

"We have to try, brother."

"We've been trying. Grev's influence is strong here. We're too far West. These villages might very well be the remnants of the first uprising. Face it, they've all fallen."

"Alright," Ragnar nodded.

"I'm sorry. We will have to make do with the men we have. Perhaps we can send some to recruit in the South. It is a shame, though, that we found no one to join us."

"We found some who would."

Adir sighed and looked over to Ragnar. He whipped his horse to begin galloping again. His younger brother following behind.

They went down the road until nightfall and then broke for camp. The moon and the light of their fire shown throughout the wooded hills. The brothers sat silently, staring into the flames. They drank out of wineskins and ate the food they had packed from their journey. An assortment of smoked meat and wrapped bread. They looked up when they heard heavy footsteps down the road.

There came a man with the resemblance of a giant. He towered over the brothers as they stood to take in the looks of this knight. In one arm, he held a half-dozen spears across his shoulders. With the other hand, he held two flails with ease. Around his waist were two swords. Over his back hung a bear pelt and a large round shield. His beard extended out from his sallet helmet, which hid all but his dark eyes.

"Hail knight," Adir raised his hand in greeting. The giant man stopped at the brothers' camp.

"Hail," The knight spoke low and slowly.

"I have not heard of a man with such stature. Surely not one who wonders with his own arsenal. Tell me then, who are you? Where, I fear, are you going?"

"I am Bramus the Conqueror. Lord of Frostford."

"Lord of Frostford?" Ragnar asked. "What are you doing out here?"

"I am the keeper of my land. And I have been told two Clansman have been going throughout my villages. Trying to recruit an army for Gabel."

Ragnar and Adir exchanged looks.

"There is no denying it. You Northerners all look the same, war savages. Not to mention your royal seals. There's a bounty out for those stray knights of Gabel. Now, prepare yourselves like men. I would fight you," Bramus took the spears and stuck them in the ground. He armed himself with the shield and held the two flails in his massive hand.

Adir went to his suit and began arming himself. Ragnar walked up behind him.

"You're not actually going to fight this man?"

"I did not earn the name 'Adir the Mighty' for nothing."

"He will kill you," Ragnar whispered.

"Brother be quick to ready the horses," Adir put on his helmet as he walked towards his challenger. He pulled his sword from its sheath and readied himself. Bramus plowed forward with his shield and brought his flails straight down. Adir turned to the side. The heavy ball and chains cratered the dirt. Bramus picked the flails back up and spung them above his head. Adir took a step back as Bramus advanced and swung across. Adir lurched and cut up at Bramus's exposed arm. The giant man bashed Adir back with his shield and brought the flails across. The heavy steel glancing off his bracer. Adir winced in pain but swung with his sword to counter. The blade rang off of Bramus's shield. Adir attacked again as Bramus sweeped his flails. The chains wrapped around his steel blade. Bramus brought his weapons back, ripping the sword from Adir's hand. Adir the Mighty brought his fists up as Bramus again began to swing the flails overhead.

"Ragnar, your hammer!" Adir shouted without taking his eyes off Bramus. His younger brother, mounted on his horse, tossed over his warhammer. Just as Adir was reaching out to catch it Bramus went to strike. Adir batted the flails out of the way as he caught the hammer. Then he swung down and crushed Bramus's shin. The lord fell to one knee and screamed in pain. He whipped the flails around, but Adir walked backwards out of range. The heavy steel denting the ground.

"Coward!" Bramus yelled.

"Next time, you will die," Adir said as he mounted his horse. The two brothers took off down the road. After some struggle, Bramus pushed himself back up to his feet. He grabbed two of his spears and broke them in half. Using their wooden poles, he made a splint. Able to stand again, Bramus started his slow march, continuing eastward after them.

The army of Saint George had filled the stone walls of the village. The men were still training in the square, some learning to shoot a bow, others to wield a sword. Smiths worked steadily to fashion arms and armor with what material they had. Sven went to the gate to meet Ragnar and Adir as they rode into the village that morning.

"It's magnificent, isn't it? Nearly a whole battalion! Men from the South and the East and even some from the North. This is the embodiment of true loyalty. All these brave souls ready to give hell to that bastard!"

"We're sorry we could not send more your way," Adir said from atop his horse.

"I think we'll have enough to siege the castle. Don't you?" Sven asked.

"Remember, we will have to overtake Fort Redmont first. They have fallen to Grev's hand and they will be waiting for us. You have high spirits, but perhaps we must take this civil war more cautiously," Adir warned.

Ragnar added on, "We will not be able to just strut up to Grev and take back the throne. Know this will be bloody. Grev couldn't have grabbed power so easily if he didn't have a strong army of his own. We met one of his lords on the road. No doubt he has more pawns to throw at us. He shouldn't be underestimated, nor should we expect him to follow the rules of war. He has no compassion for his enemies, we should have none for him. They have mages, too. No telling what witchcraft they'll use against us."

"But we will be ready," Sven turned to the men all training in the yard. Adir looked on, but only sighed at the sight. Archers were struggling to place arrows on their targets. Swordsmen were swinging recklessly. "You look like you're grieving for them."

"I am," Adir replied as he got off his horse. "They're not ready. They need more time."

"Don't doubt us, now. Men with a passion are dangerous in battle. Even if they don't know it yet," Sven walked them deeper into the fort.

"We best hope you're right," Ragnar said.

Night came, and the village still glowed with torch light and the fire of the forges still burning. Guards were plentiful along the stone walls. Tents occupied the fields inside and out of the village. Most had their own little fires where men were talking to each other.

"Sir! A rider is approaching!" One of the guardsmen yelled to his officer. The forest was dark at night and this rider's face couldn't be seen. "Who goes there?" The guard called as he neared the gate. Others along the wall readied their bows and took aim at this night rider.

"Who is your King?" The horseman asked.

"High King Gabel!" The guard shouted.

"I am the son of whom you fight for! I am Ivan, Son of Gabel, Son of Gunder. Prince of the Realms and heir to the throne!" The rider called up to the guard. Immediately they lowered their weapons and rushed down to meet him.

"Apologies your highness," The guard's torch reflected off Ivan's black armor. In the light, the men could see the young prince wearing his silver circlet. His face grimaced as he tried to hold back the pain. "What happened to you?"

"I tried to fight him," Ivan said.

"Grev?"

"Aye. I must see the royal knights at once. I heard they were here."

"Two of them. I'll fetch them to you. Get yourself patched up, lad," One guard took off.

The other led Ivan to the healer's tent. The prince had his armor removed and was laid down on a bunk. The healer held his hands over Ivan and closed his eyes as he focused his energy on the wounds.

"Your highness," Ragnar said as he went through the tent. Adir following behind. The healer stepped back to let Ivan sit up and see the knights.

"You do not know how good it is to see a friendly face," Ivan greeted them.

"It is good to see you as well. What is happening in the capital? We haven't heard any news, only that Grev took over and reinstated his own army."

"That and I'm afraid the news doesn't get any better. Grev, he..." Ivan swallowed the emotion, "He executed Evangeline. He's been executing people who stood up against him, my sister was brave and loyal enough to do so. Ulfer as well, was slain," Ivan shook his head. Tears streamed now from his eyes. "I-I was a coward. I gave into his facade and... I let my sister die."

"Ivan, you did what you felt you had to do to survive," Adir tried to comfort him.

"No. I didn't. I just gave in and did as he asked. I actually believed that he wasn't responsible for the attacks on my father. That he was somehow justified."

"Maybe. Hell, maybe that was the case. But by the looks of it, you stood up against him. You overcame the submission of fear," Ivan nodded, taking in Adir's words. The prince wiped his tears.

"There is something else. Grev himself is a sorcerer. He's a powerful mage. He tortured people, he could shoot fire from his palms and summon weapons at his command. It is more than anything I have seen or even heard of."

"By the divine... and you still managed to survive him in a fight?" Ragnar was shocked.

"Yes. What news of my father?" Ivan changed the subject.

"We know he escaped Grev's men. There were signs that he was in Crossroads. But the town was obliterated. Another village was sacked to the North. Sir Igran and Sir Delwyn set out for it, yet we have not heard from them since."

The prince sat back in the bunk.

"This is an impressive army you have gathered. Will they be ready?" He asked the knights.

"They are all good men, my prince. Rest now, in the morning we will discuss war."

"War is happening now, Adir," Ivan said.

"There will be no attack this night. Tomorrow, we will have you caught up," The knights left Ivan to rest and heal.

At dawn, Ivan woke and left the healer's tent. In his black doublet, he walked around the fort as it came to life. Fires already started at the forge warmed the frosty air. Soldiers' breaths could be seen as they got up to start another day of training. Mist below the fort covered the expanse, Saint George appeared to be built on the clouds. Chimes echoed through the village as hammers fell on steel. Ivan walked to see the smith who was up before the others. The rhythmic pounding of the hammer beat life into men who woke to begin their work. The prince stared at the young smith, a man about his age with long copper hair tied out of his face. Myles worked relentlessly, crafting swords the way he was taught, making the weapons to take back the kingdom. Ivan started to walk away when he noticed something on the smith's hip. A sword whose hilt could be seen from its sheath. A sword that shown like silver.

"Where did you find this blade?" Ivan walked up to him.

"Found it," Myles wiped the sweat off his forehead before returning to pound the hot steel with his hammer.

"That is my father's blade. Dawnsmist, the King's Sword."

"I found it in battle. The sword saved my life and I have not parted with it since."

"By right, it is mine," Ivan said. Myles looked up at the prince. Taking the hot steel, he dipped it in a bucket of water. Steam rushed into the air.

"You really the prince, then?"

"Yes. Now give that sword to me."

"Then why don't you take it, your highness?" Myles said as he kept working. "In a duel."

"You would have me fight you for it?"

"Unless you are scared, sire."

"It is not out of fear. That blade is mine. If anything, I would be afraid for you. Your hands may have made many swords. But that does not mean they are used to swinging one. I'll accept your duel. Should I best you, I'll take my father's sword and send word to find a new blacksmith."

"Should I win, you'll admit the sword presented itself to me and it is my right to wield."

"Very well, but neither will fight with the King's Sword. You can use one of your own that you've made. If you trust in your own craftsmanship."

Ivan left to retrieve his weapon from the healer's. Myles took off his apron and wiped his face off with a rag.

Choosing one of his own swords arbitrarily, he twirled it around to feel its weight and balance. The smith then walked out to the field that lay between the forge and the healer's tent. Prince Ivan sat on a stool and had the healer dress him in his armor.

"Leaving for battle already?" Adir asked as he saw the prince. He turned to see Myles in the opening staring them down. "What in the blazes is going on?"

"A duel. That boy has my father's sword. I am to win it back," Ivan replied as he moved his shoulders to get a feel for the armor.

"That 'boy' is older than you. Look, this is nonsense."

"That sword is all I have of my father right now."

"You have his strength, too. But remember who your enemy is."

"I know," Ivan stood and took his sword and discarded the sheath. "But right now, it's him," Ivan began to walk intently toward Myles, who was pacing slowly on the other side of the field. Adir shook his head and followed behind. "Have you no armor, smith?" Ivan called over.

"I was not blessed to have a suit made of gold for me. My skills are the only defense I'll need."

"We will see if that holds true."

Both of them outstretched their blade and slowly inched towards the other. As soon as they tapped swords, Ivan brought his weapon overhead and chopped down. Myles directed it to the side, then turned his blade up. Ivan brought his sword back around to counter. The steel blades scraped each other as they rotated. Ivan pushed his opponent's sword away then swung at him in a flurry. Myles had his blade up and blocked each incoming attack. As Ivan charged forward, Myles stepped to the side and elbowed the prince in the nose.

Ivan turned back, stabbing his sword forward. Myles turned his blade down to block. Then brought his sword up to return attacks. Myles now stepped forward with each swing, Ivan walking back as he blocked the attacks. The prince put two hands on the hilt and swung across. Myles took the opening and struck Ivan in the arm. The blade ringing off the armor. Ivan swung down and across several times, cutting at Myles in an 'X' pattern. Myles thrusted his sword at the prince, but it was blocked by this continuous sweeping.

As Ivan stepped forward and swung down, Myles blocked up with his sword and kicked out Ivan's foot. Off balance, the prince fell back in his heavy armor. The prince lifted his head up from the grass. Myles pointed his blade between the prince's eyes. Ragnar and Sven emerged from the mead hall to see this.

"What are you doing?" Ragnar ran over. Adir put his hand up to quietly stop his brother.

"Truly," Ivan said, staring down the blade of his opponent. "That sword belongs to you."

Myles dropped his sword and extended his hand. The prince paused before accepting the gesture. Myles pulled Ivan up to his feet, straining from the weight of the armor.

"I would be honored to wield it in your father's name," Myles said. Ivan let out a sigh then went to hug him.

"He's all I have left. Know he means the world to me."

"That's not so," Myles said.

"Excuse me?"

"He is not all you have left. Your sister is very much alive," Ivan took a few steps back after hearing this.

"What do you mean? She was executed. Grev told me."

"Yes, he did. He wanted you each to believe the other was dead. I overheard his men in the forest. The princess, your sister, is alive."

The Sorcerer

Through the slopes of the Red Mountains, Grev was taken across Three Mile March to Farfair Hold. There were no signs of that long-ago battle. Grass grew where fire had once consumed the mountain. The stone ruins at the base of the mountain had been built up with sharp towers and thick walls. Guards in violet opened the metal gates to let the carriage pass.

Grev stepped out of the cart and made his way across the rocky ground. Around him the great fort was being reconstructed. Dwarves worked endlessly, with shackles around their feet, to rebuild their ancient hold. Halls were added between the towers and large corridors were being made to fill the hollow ruins. A large circular courtyard was already completed between the unfinished buildings. It held several tall statues of cloaked figures, circling around the dead bushes below.

Grev walked past all this and went down a set of stairs that dove into the mountain. Plinks rang through the cavern as dwarves dug into the stone with pickaxes. They cut huge blocks from the stone and would each carry one on their back, bringing them to the surface to build more of the fortress. The dwarves were grimy and roughly dressed. The chains around their feet dragged on the ground as they worked. Their beards were long and knotted and their eyes looked sore and tired.

"*Hvor mar rlokk måsch grav? De rød fjellan esch noch tilhører dem.*"

"*Vær stel, dverg. Omand heir esch-*"

Their human taskmaster cracked his whip at the two speaking. None of the workers flinched at this but kept digging in silence.

"*Bek ker,*" The first softly said to the other. On the far side of the cave, other dwarves beat their hammers as they forged nails and picks. The cave was filled with the heat of the furnace. One worker shoveled in coal and pushed on the billows to keep the fire at melting heat.

"*Jeer smed esch noch bryte ruggen. Noch gåttered som oss gravbeger,*" One miner grumbled at the blacksmith.

Grev walked past the dwarves without paying any mind and went to the end of the tunnel. The clanging of metal echoed down a shaft that fell straight into the depths of the earth. A dwarf stood near with a torch. He was only half the height of the old man, charcoal colored beard, and bushy eyebrows. His square boots were torn through, most other dwarves simply worked bare foot. Grev heard the sound of the taskmaster cracking his whip again but didn't so much as turn to look.

"Send up the lift," Grev ordered. The dwarf cranked on a wheel connected to endless rope and a series of pullies. He reeled up a wooden elevator and handed Grev his torch. The old man shook as he stepped onto the wooden lift, dangling above the abyss. Slowly the dwarf turned the crank the other way. The lift jolted as it started to move and Grev descended into the deep. The mine walls were close on all sides of the lift. Some points the rock face was out of reach, other points, the wooden lift would be scrapped as it went along.

The shaft then opened up into a great chasm. The elevator practically being lowered into a great, black nothingness. The torch that shone off the surrounding rocks now only faintly lit an aura around the dusty atmosphere. Eventually, the torchlight reflected a stone floor. It was the same dark rock as the rest of the mountain. The wooden lift landed abruptly, knocking the old man off balance.

"Damn dwarf," He said to himself as he stepped off the lift. His torch picked up more of the cave floor now. The slate was cold and sharp. In the distance were great natural pillars holding up the mountain from within. Grev proceeded into the chasm, shuffling in his dark robes. Out of the silence, sharp coughs echoed off the ancient walls. Grev turned but could see no one.

He walked past these great pillars, extending high into the unseen ceiling. Grev walked until he neared the back wall of the cave which was perfectly cut from the jagged black rock. The smooth wall extended higher than he could see and was even longer in width. At the middle of this wall was a man who was joined with the rock. His torso pushing out was the only blemish to the wall. His legs and arms were sealed behind him. Only his face was truly exposed, but even then, rocks grew on his brow and on his lips. He had a long dusty beard and bald head. He let out another sharp cough as Grev approached him.

"Grevok. It has been so long."

"Tyrus," Grev greeted.

"I've felt rumbling from the surface. You have created quite some chaos, my student."

"Only what is necessary to overturn this flawed world."

"Be careful trying to turn over the world or you might find yourself dwelling below *me*."

"I did not come down here for this banter."

"What could you possibly come to gain? You were the one who claimed to have surpassed me."

"I need more power," Grev answered.

"More power? Haven't you enough? You have a crown on your head and the world trembling at your feet."

"No," He snapped. "I was nearly defeated in a duel against the prince. How could I wish to outmatch the King if his boy son could almost kill me?"

"Hmph... His lineage must be truly divine if even you still refer to him as King."

"Enough!" Grev's voiced carried across the chasm.

"You are out of luck, I'm afraid. You are nearing the end of your magic."

"That cannot be," Grev replied.

"You have much power over the flame, but if you wish to cross any further, it will consume you. Your magic comes at a price, my student. A cost for defiling the gift."

"Don't give me that jargon."

"Believe what you want, we both know casting Western Magics take a toll on the body. The more powerful a spell, the more costly it is to you. Soon enough, if you grow any more powerful, your spells would be lethal to yourself. It would kill your soul."

"I've seen you do much more powerful things than I and yet you did not die. And somehow refuse to die even now," Grev thought.

"So, what's the secret?" Tyrus asked rhetorically. "You cannot change the amount a spell taxes you."

"Then you must change how much a soul can take..."

"You're getting it now. Your soul is mortal and weak. As powerful as you are, Grevok, it is the same size spirit as everyone else's."

"Would I need someone else's? Or a different kind of soul?"

"Yes... A different kind. One strong enough to withstand the magic you intend to cast. A soul that can be *ignited*."

"What do you mean ignited?"

"That is the threshold you are attempting to pass. Complete mastery of fire. Not just summoning weapons or shooting meteors, but actual dominance. Your very essence would be ignited, inferno."

"How then do I do this?"

"What beast do you know of has complete mastery over fire? That is the soul you would need."

"A dragon? You expect me to vanquish a dragon?"

"If you cannot do that, then you are not powerful enough to need go further."

"Is that what you did, teacher? Take a soul from a dragon?"

"It is what's kept me alive. Dragons are undying. They can only be killed; they do not age like mortals."

"So, I could still be killed?"

Tyrus coughed, dust escaping his lungs.

"You will be the most powerful wizard on the surface of the Realms if you are not already. If you worry so much about dying, then I do not think you fit."

"Do not forget who put you in here," Grev said.

"Do not forget I could let myself out because we both know I will always be more powerful than you!" As Tyrus spoke violet lightning flashed between his teeth and shot from his eyes. Grev took a step back. "I have told you what is required of you, my student."

Grev turned and walked away from the man in the stone. Sharp coughs echoed into the chasm as Grev hurried to the lift.

In the empty streets of Castle Rock, the final defacements were being made. Men worked with picks and rope to bring down the great Watchman of the Realms. The giant statue was broken at the feet and fell onto the streets near the castle gates. The great marble shattered and took buildings down with it. The rubble was left in the street. Most had already moved out of the city in fear of Grev's tyranny. Riding slowly between the rubble, two cloaked men made their way up to the castle. Grev was in the courtyard when they arrived, watching the red and gold banners burning on the ground.

"What is it?" Grev asked.

"Our scouts have figured out where the resistance is mustering," Barris reported.

"Well?" He asked.

"In the Highland Realm. Saint George, sir," Bosa answered.

"If these farmers want to wage war against us, let the bastards come! We will quell them in their efforts."

"Most certainly, your highness," Bosa said.

"I was on the royal court for a great many years, listening to endless debates. All the King's noblemen would just talk. Now look what's become of them," Grev pointed to the burning banners. "I was the only one in the damned court who was willing to do anything. And Gabel hated me for it, as much as his peasants do now. I wanted a more powerful Realm, a greater kingdom. Those who still think this power is unlawful, were never fit to live in this kingdom in the first place. It was them who held us back, kept us weak. Yes, let them form an army. Let them see firsthand the power my kingdom will hold."

"I shall send word to Captain Ballard. His fort is most immediate to Saint George. We will crush this resistance, as you have commanded, my king," Barris said.

"Give them not a swift death. Each soul should suffer long enough to comprehend their mistake. Power and might, men."

"Power and might, my king," They bowed. The two soldiers got back to their horses and rode off, echoing down the empty street.

Grev left the fires burning and walked up the steps into the great hall. It was dim and empty inside. Nothing but the throne remained from the previous Kings.

"I am running out of time. The King will be upon us soon enough," Grev said to himself. "I need to find a dragon quickly, but where?" He slammed his fist against a pillar as he walked by. Grev looked up and saw the throne at the end of the hall. He gazed at it for some time before he remembered a certain young knight. A knight who wanted justice for his village, who wanted a dragon slain.

"Guard," He hollered, figuring someone was in an earshot of him. A soldier in purple came from around the corner.

"Yes, lord?"

"Get the carriage."

"Yes, lord," The guard ran out of the hall.

Not long after, Grev walked out of the castle and awaited his ride. Grev pulled himself into his carriage as it pulled up by the inner wall.

"Thundertree," Grev called up to the driver and they began to move. He took a small potion and braced himself for the bumpy ride out of the city.

Grev's carriage stopped in the middle of a misty road. Deep forests surrounded them on all sides. A knock came from the carriage window.

"We're here, sire."

Grev closed his eyes, breathed deeply, then pushed open the door. The old man stepped onto a cobble road that paved its way through the Avarwood and led to this ruined village. Pale stone walls were collapsed onto the road, preventing the horses from going any further. Other buildings further up were caved in on themselves, but what remained was a tall stone keep. Birds chirped from the empty trees as all the leaves had fallen for the season. The stones were frosted over and Grev could see his own breath in the cold day. He walked around the ruins of the wall and entered the desecrated village. From the broken glass of the keep, he could see large scales of green. Grev tilted his head to try to get a size for the beast.

"Should we stay here, sir?" One of his armed guards called over. The three of them were fully armored and ready with halberds.

"Shh," Grev hissed. He put his finger up to his ear, telling the men to listen. There was a low, soft rumble, but after looking around Grev concluded it was the creaking of trees in the wind. He waved for the guards come to him. They slowly climbed over the rubble and pressed their backs against the outside of the keep. Grev peered into the window once more then scanned the outside of the keep. There was an opening near the back corner. Grev shuffled over to it. His guards watched him carefully. He pointed at one of them and motioned toward the front door. The soldier nodded and proceeded around to the front.

The guard became shaky as he rounded the corner. As he looked in, he could only see a long emerald tail. He followed it sharply along the wall to see a dragon in mid breath. He stumbled backwards out of the keep as a ray of fire shot through the old wooden doors. The other guards ran around to meet him. The dragon's head went through the doorway, biting down at its fleeing prey. The guards threw up their halberds and stabbed the creature. It flinched and blow fire down on the earth, the flames quickly blowing outward. The dragon pulled back into the keep and threw down its wings, taking flight inside the large stone structure. But as it flew up a chain was wrapped around its tail. It turned sharply to see Grev, pulling down on the magical chain he had summoned. The dragon sprayed fire at him, but the old mage waved his hand and dispelled the dragon's flames. Shooting his hand up, he shot his own dark fire at the creature. The dragon roared and shook off the fire that blasted its head.

The dragon landed back on the ground and stomped in rage before breathing more fire at Grev. As its head was turned, one of the guards ran in and stabbed the beast between the claws of its toes. It roared and swung its tail, the guard shattering into a window. Grev whipped the dragon with his chain. As he went to strike again, the chain wrapped around the dragon's snout. It huffed smoke from its nostrils and threw its head around. Grev's chain was ripped from his hands and when the dragon unhinged its jaws to break free, the chain shattered and dispersed.

The dragon stooped down and clawed its way into the spiral stairs of the keep's tower. The stone steps broke under its weight as the dragon climbed to reach the tower's summit. Grev ran behind and jumped across what steps were left to follow with the dragon. He shot fire up at his fleeing enemy. Its tail whipping around in the tower, trying to strike back. Grev conjured another dark chain, he wrapped it around his hand as it was summoned, then he threw it to catch the dragon's tail. The green dragon pulled the old man up to top of the tower. It broke through the ceiling with the spread of its wings, roaring as it did so. Flocks of birds scattered from the trees they towered over.

Grev, standing on top of the tower with the dragon, lashed out with his chain, cutting into the creature's soft belly. It breathed fire on him, but the wizard directed the flames to pass around him. Summoning his flaming sword now, Grev stabbed the dragon in the gut. His fire now burning the dragon from the inside. It screamed and stood up on its hind legs, then clawed down with its front.

"Give me your soul, dragon!" Grev yelled. With one hand, he reached out toward the beast, the other on his own chest. Twisting his fingers, he pulled a dark essence from the beast. It roared in excruciating pain as the weakened dragon was near dying. Grev pulled its soul closer into himself, then the hand on his chest lifted up and started to take his own soul from his body. Grev screamed now too, trying to concentrate through the torment this spell was costing. Then with one motion, he brought the dragon's soul into his chest and shot his own soul out into the dragon. The beast quickly fell back off the tower and died as it hit the ground.

Grev looked at his shaking hand as a new strength filled his body. The feeling of magma now surged through his blood. He stood up and roared, breathing fire straight into the air. Flames surrounded him in the image of a dragon. Wings of fire and a tail grew off his back and fiery claws overlapped his hands. As the image of the dragon burned up and dispelled, his eyes remained on fire for a short while. Then breathing deeply, Grev dispelled all his magic and stood with grin on his face. He summoned his wings of fire again and glided down the tower, back into the keep. Smoke and embers trailed behind him. The man landed softly on the settling rubble and quickly let his wings burn themselves up.

"You killed it," His guards met him as Grev was walking back to the carriage.

"I became it," He replied and stepped into the carriage. "Now let's move. We have a King to kill."

The Castle

Across the Realm, the knights and villagers rode east into the Avarwood. The Northern stretch of the forest was dark with ancient pines, birch, and oaks that held a great span of leaves that covered the earth from getting any sunlight. Green, gold, and red filled the plants around them. The horses tore up the dirt as they rode hard through the woods. They kicked through layers of fallen leaves. They rode over wide rivers, the Wayfarer leading the men to shallow points to cross. They were led up holts and down through vales.

"Have we missed it?" Igran stopped his horse.

"Do you accuse me of misguiding you?" Otstyr asked, sitting on the horse with Delwyn.

"Don't you smell it?" Igran turned to the men. "He's led us all the way to the sea. The priest told us it was within the forest and here, you've ridden us passed it."

"Do not accuse me, sir knight, of misplacing something *you* have never found. This fortress lies on the Great Sea. If you can smell the salt in the mist then we are close."

"Carry on," Igran pulled his horse back for Delwyn and Otstyr to lead the way. They rode further toward the smell of the sea. Beyond the dense forest of gold and green, was a horizon of blue. The horses stopped when they reached the rocky shoreline. Large square stones formed the cliffs and shores along the sea. The grey water that crashed onto them looked endless.

From the peninsula the knights emerged on, they saw an island. A small island with pines and autumn leaves. Lay safely hidden in the trees was a keep. It was humble in size, a strong square base with one tower rising from that, only twice as tall as the pines below. The old keep was of pale stone with vines growing up the walls.

"Behold, Castle Unknown," Otstyr pointed to the lone keep. The island only a hundred yards or so off the shore.

"This old fort is Castle Unknown?" Fergus asked.

"Yes. Built by the Fervent Knights of old. This fortress has always served as a secret retreat in such an emergency. Make no mistake it will be guarded."

"Hitch the horses," Igran turned to the others. He dismounted and led his horse to be tied up.

"Are we to swim?" One of the villagers asked.

"You may do as you wish. I'm taking the boat," Igran gestured down the stone beach to a longboat that was moored. The men rowed their way to the island. The boat rolling over the water. Saltwater sprayed into the air was they rowed against the waves. They beached the longboat and tied it to a pine tree growing out of the water. Approaching the fort, they heard no sound. No torches to be seen on the walls or inside the dark windows.

"No one's here," Delwyn's voice echoed across the island. The men stood near the dark wooden entrance.

Lochlan approached the door, but an arrow whizzed from atop the keep.

"The hell!" He called out, staring at the arrow between his feet.

"Name the ground you stand," The archer's voice rang out. The men peered up the tower but saw no one.

"What?" Another arrow sank into the rocky ground.

"Name the ground you stand."

"This is Castle Unknown!" Igran shouted back. "The very place of our King!"

There came no reply. The knights looked to each other and readied their weapons. Moments later, the ancient door creaked open. Two knights in white cloaks appeared.

"Come quickly now," Cedric said. The men followed inside, and the door was shut and barred behind them. The dim keep was only lit by the sunlight peering through the black-framed windows. "Follow brother Edwards," The older knight said.

The white knight walked the men through the dark corridor and up several flights of stairs to the top of the keep. They were led into a room which had a balcony overlooking the Great Sea. Standing on the balcony was an older man, hunched over the railing as he watched the horizons.

"My liege," Edwards spoke soft to get the man's attention, bowing his head as he did so. The greying red-haired noble turned from his over watch and faced the men. Although he was old, he was still strong in appearance.

"My King," Igran bent his knee in allegiance, the others did the same.

"My knights," Gabel sighed. "Rise. We surely have much to discuss."

The King and his men went down a flight of stairs to the dining hall. The room was the same pale grey stone that made up the entire fort. Thin windows and several unlit torches lined the walls. They sat around a long wooden table in the middle of the room.

"An army is forming over in Saint George," Igran began. "Hardy men from the nearby realms have gone there to help fight. The army is simply there waiting for your command. Each day, their numbers grow but surely Grev's does too. If we make haste for Saint George, you could take charge of this army."

The King shook his head.

"That will not be enough. Perhaps we have a few hundred farmers, but they will not last against the prowess of Grev's men. It has dawned on me that we are in need of *real* fighters. This kingdom hasn't had the need of an army since we last vanquished the Army of the West. Guardsmen is all we've had. Perhaps we Kings were not ignorant to have an army at the ready in case of trials such as this. For there is an army now we can call upon. The orcs in the North."

"No," Igran protested. "I will not work with those monsters."

"They have armies of the best trained fighters. And they are still under rule of the kingdom. Yes, orcs and men have fought, but their chief owes his allegiance to the

King. There is no army better and more feared than the orcs."

"No army better?! Men with a fire in their hearts, fighting for their homeland are far better than hired muscle!"

"Dammit, Igran, set aside your hatred! This is about the whole kingdom, do not be selfish in this. Men have done far worse to each other than what the orcs have done to you. As hard as that is to see, you must put that behind you. Sir Delwyn, too sought vengeance, but gave that up for the greater good!" Gabel shouted. They all sat in silence for a moment.

"Say we do go to the Orcish people," Igran begun. "What of the army we have called in Saint George?"

"I am not suggesting we get rid of them, but we cannot win this war on the backs of farmers alone," Gabel reassured. "Forgive me, I do not mean to underestimate the army you have rallied for me. But we need go to the orcs for reinforcement. They are a warring people and are unmatched in battle. This is their kingdom too; they will answer our calls."

"Aye, we should send the villagers back to the Army of Saint George, tell them of our movements. Sven, their lord, and commander shall take charge of this army. He can campaign his men through the villages that fell to Grev's rule," Delwyn suggested.

"I agree, yet they should not try to siege Castle Rock until our company has marched south, that way we can meet them and combine forces for the attack," Igran added.

"Let it be so," King Gabel commanded. Igran nodded and turned to leave.

In the early morning, Edwards rose and slipped out from the hall to go to the front door. Crickets could be heard chirping from outside the pale walls.

"Where are you off to?" Cedric came down the stairs.

"Nowhere."

"Brother, do not leave us now."

"You heard the King's men. They're going for an army. They don't need us anymore. I'm going back to Sanctuary."

"Our town is gone, Edwards. There is no Sanctuary. I'm sorry, they're gone."

"We should have never left them," The young Fervent knight took his hand off the door. "We should have stayed to fight for them."

"We would have died, too. You know we fight only for one cause."

"What does that mean? What good is it to say we fight for our God and then let his holy city fall? The last place in the Realms where people knew his name. Was not that our fight? Instead, we listen to orders: protect the King. Surely he is more valuable than hundreds of lives."

"Edwards, enough," Cedric scolded. "You swore an oath to this order. Do not forget that."

"What good is it to be fervent for our God if no good comes of it? To devote ourselves to this holy order and bring no good into this world, purge it of no evil?"

"Are you doubting our task or our God?" The older knight asked. Edwards shuttered.

"I do not want to be a Fervent knight anymore."

"As soon as you no longer want to be fervent, you're not," Cedric said.

Edwards looked away for a moment and shook his head lightly. He slowed his breathing before speaking again.

"I do still believe we can serve Adonai," He said. "But not like this. We've done him no good."

"God does not need *us* to do good," Cedric said. "He very well may be working for good in this darkness. All he asks us is to be faithful to him."

"And I will stay faithful. But if there is no one out there left who knows his name, then I think our purpose is clear."

"Our purpose?" The old knight asked.

"Cedric, the King does not need our help anymore. We did what we were asked. I know there's nothing we can do about home. But now, I'd say we have a new quest. Tell the people of their God. Brother, if you're with me, I would be honored to serve with you."

Cedric sighed and thought for a minute.

"You're right. I will call on the other knights. We would go with you. But you will tell the King."

"Alright," Edwards nodded. Cedric turned to go back up the stairs. He paused after a few steps and turned back.

"Edwards."

"Yes?"

"You are fervent," Cedric said before ascending up the steps to the keep.

After a few hours, the other men were up and walking about the cool stone keep. The two men who came from Saint George were preparing to go back to their village and to send the news to Sven. Igran came down from the keep and was putting his bag in the boat as well.

"Igran," Gabel called to his knight from a few yards off. "I beg you; you must come with us. I understand where you come from, but we are in a greater need. Our kingdom has fallen, and I need the few good men we have close to me."

"You have the holy knights to protect you," Igran gestured to the keep.

"They're leaving, too. It's just us now."

"How can I go and fight with the people who killed my wife?" Igran asked. "How can you ask me to do that?"

"The orc that killed her is dead. Do not forget that men pillaged and killed orcs, as well. They too lost family, were widowed, yet that doesn't mean that our two peoples must be enemies. I beg you; I need my trusted knights close to me."

Igran sighed, lifted his gear out of the boat, and set it on the ground. Fergus and Lochlan then pushed off and rowed back to the rocky shore.

The King

At Castle Unknown, the King and his loyal knights prepared for their travels to the Orcish Realm, a rugged region of steep mountains and dark forests. The torches in the keep were snuffed out and the old stone building looked again as it had been abandoned for ages. The Fervent knights in their white cloaks had already taken their boat to the mainland and had ridden off into the woods.

"The ride out of the forest and around the bay will take four days at least. No telling the length it will take us to hike the mountain pass to Oorog," King Gabel prompted his men.

"If I may…" Otstyr, the old creature began. "Perhaps we shall go by sea, take the bay across. Tis quicker. Less threat of finding Grev's men who may occupy the land. We do not know how many villages in that passage have fallen. It would be wiser pass undetected by water."

"Where did you find this one?" Gabel asked Igran.

"Hiding in the Red Mountains. He said he worked for King Gunder."

"You'd have to be really old, friend, to have known Gunder," Gabel looked down at him.

"I do not have to show you the way. I have fulfilled my end of bringing you here. Yes, I knew King Gunder. I made the map of the whole Realms that hangs in the great hall. I have always been loyal to your kingdom."

"Alright," Igran said. "It is up to you, my King."

"Would I gain from lying to men with swords taller than me?" The old Wayfarer asked.

"You will lead us to Oorog," Gabel said.

"As you wish," The Wayfarer bowed.

They rowed back from the island and went to retrieve their horses. Their animals galloped onwards, north through the darker part of the forest. The Wayfarer noted each landmark as they made their turns. A fallen tree, a boulder, a forest troll den. The clouds rolled in from the sea as they rode along the woods.

They found their way out of the forest and went along the road now to the city of Haul. It was dusk when they drew near and the fog was thick near the bay, which was named the Orcish Lake. Across the bay of jagged rocks, stood the great Dawn Mountains, tallest peaks in all the Realms. At this point, they remained unseen behind the drizzling fog. The city's walls were high and gated by a heavy wooden portcullis. Crows swooped down from the trees to caw and mock the earth.

"Who goes there?" A guard called from the mist, only hearing the horses approach. His torch light could be seen from the top of the city wall.

"Hold, sire," Otstyr said as Gabel was approaching the gate. "Might I suggest we keep ourselves hidden. There is another entrance."

"You are fortunate you are wise. Most don't get away with ordering a King," Gabel replied. Otstyr led the horses and quietly walked them around the city wall. The mist kept the men hidden as the snuck to a secret port. Otstyr stopped when he reached a brush pile up against the city wall. Igran got off his horse and helped the old creature move the debris away. Behind the soaked branches was a narrow door.

"This was built as a way to smuggle goods in and out of the city," Otstyr informed the men as he moved the brush away from the door. The door opened into a dark tunnel.

"Interesting," Igran distastefully as he opened the door. The dimly lit tunnel was short enough to see the other end. The men followed the Wayfarer as he approached this next door. Otstyr peered through the cracks of the wood, then opened the latch of the door. The King's men found themselves in the back room of a dusty inn. The few dreary folks who were inside didn't seem to care that men were coming out of the tunnel. Though the dirty suits of chainmail and surcoats were surely out of place.

"You'll have refuge here for the night. The ferry won't go across till morning," Otstyr said.

"Can we be sure this is safe?" Delwyn asked.

"You're the most heavily armed ones in the place. I'd say you're fine," Otstyr walked to the bartender. The two spoke quietly. The barrel-chested man behind the counter glanced over at the knights, still in the doorway of this back room.

"I don't like this," Igran said under his breath. Otstyr returned with the man close behind.

"Follow me," The man grunted. Gabel nodded and the three men followed the bartender up a flight of stairs and into a bunk room. "You can hide out here for the night. My old friend here can fill you in on my policy: you get caught, it's not my problem."

"Sir," Gabel stopped him as he was leaving. The King took out three gold coins. "Fetch us some cloaks and we'll be less of a problem."

"Right away, sire," The man nodded and took the gold.

"Rest up," Gabel addressed his knights as they were already unstrapping their armor. "We'll have to leave early tomorrow. And Igran, go find where that creature went."

"Yes sir," The knight tied his sheath back around his waist and went out the room. Going down the stairs, he looked around the inn. Otstyr was nowhere to be seen. There was a faint bell going off outside. Igran went closer to the window and peered into the city streets but saw nothing. The bartender rushed in with cloaks folded up in his arms.

"Here you go, sir," He handed one to Igran.

"Oh, thanks," He grabbed it, his focus was still on the ringing bell. The man went up the stairs to deliver the other cloaks. Igran threw his cloak on and stepped out into the rainy streets. He weaved his way through the tight buildings and found himself following along the city wall. As he neared the gate, he heard more commotion. Guards were running past and rallying on the streets. Their armor clanked like the thunder overhead. Peering around the front gate, Igran saw rows of soldiers standing in the mist. Soldiers in purple sashes.

"Get out of here," One guard waved Igran off. The portcullis of the gate was dropped shut. Each army now standing off, waiting for orders.

"Surrender now, and no one will be harmed," One of the officers yelled to the town guards. Yet the guards did not ease from their posts.

Igran ran back through the alleys of brick buildings back to the inn. He rushed up the stairs and into the bunkroom.

"The city is under attack," Igran said.

"What?" Gabel stood from his seat.

"We should go. Delwyn, suit up."

"You suggest we run?" Gabel asked his knight.

"There is a chance the city's guards will be overtaken. But if Grev's men know you're here, they will not spare this place. They've leveled every village thus far that they've suspected you were hiding in. My King, it is advantageous we stay hidden. We can flee back out the passage."

"No," Gabel said. "I will not run. If we fight with them, we could save this city from falling."

"We go now, we can take it back when we have our army," Igran suggested.

"At how many lives? No. I will not hide. Let them know the King is here and he will have providence over his kingdom. Take up arms my men," Gabel grabbed the bronze greatsword. "We are going to battle."

"Very well," Igran nodded and the knights suited up again. The King was still without armor. With swords in hand, the men went down the steps of the inn and out into city. Rain was continuing to drop, and thunder filled the sky with the continuous warning bell. The three ran through puddles in the streets to where the guards were rallied. The Army of the West brought timbers to try and push the portcullis back open. Guards were against the heavy gate warding off the soldiers on the other side with spears.

"Fire!" The captain of the guard ordered, and a barrage of arrows were released. Archers fired from both sides, sending arrows flying up and down the city walls.

"Again!" The captain ordered as archers nocked their bowstrings with more arrows.

"Open the gate!" Gabel's voice boomed over the guards. They turned and looked at him.

"We don't take orders from civilians!" The captain of the guard called down from the city walls.

"I am the King in whom your city stands for. Fight with me!" Gabel walked to the portcullis and stared his enemies down. He and his knights holding their swords at the ready. The soldiers outside staggered back in his presence. "Open the gate," Gabel said once more.

Guards rushed to obey. They cranked the wheel. Chains pulled the heavy portcullis back into the air. As soon as it lifted from the ground, Gabel, the knights, and all the guards behind them charged forward with a great shout. Their voices carried with the storm. Their swords mowed through the first line of spearmen, quickly dispersing their defensive position.

Lightning and thunder roared in the sky as the men below yelled and fought in the mud. Guards fought with swords as their comrades continued to shower arrows from above. The rows of Grev's soldiers quickly widened to attack in a semicircle around them. They pressed in with their spears, stabbing some of the guards before they could even reach.

"They've pinned us!" One guard yelled.

"Follow me!"

Gabel swung the greatsword around and cut down one of the oncoming spearmen. His sword able to reach as far as his enemy's spears. The old King struck with full swings, the great weapon sweeping over the battle, breaking up their lines. The bronze stood out like the sun from the weapons of steel it clashed against. Guards came up behind him and began to fight outward from the opening he created. They struck the spearmen from the sides, eventually turning their well organized formation into chaos.

Sir Delwyn pushed forward into the fight. The muddy ground slipping beneath him. Rain shook off his armor as a spear struck against his kite shield. He then used his shield to push the spear out of the way and stabbed out with his sword. Piercing his opponent through his chainmail. Delwyn pulled his sword back then chopped downward for the kill. Another soldier grabbed his shield and drove it to the ground, twisting the knight's arm. Delwyn slashed across, but his opponent backstepped to dodge then kicked him to the ground with his steel boot.

Igran came from his side and swatted the enemy's spear away. Yet as soon as he saved Delwyn, he moved on to other opponents. Sir Igran was skillful and quick with the longsword. He blocked attacks and countered when he saw an opening. The experienced knight redirected the spears jabbing out at him, forcing them to the ground then quickly cutting up at their wielders. Rain ran down from his short black hair and was wicked off his face with his sharp movements. Igran struck his opponents down with the sword in his right hand then passed it to his left to attack enemies on the other side.

Delwyn pushed up from the ground, his shield stuck beneath the mud. With two hands now on his sword, Delwyn dueled his attackers. He chopped down, breaking a wooden spear as it was stabbed toward him. The soldier raised up what was left in his defense, blocking Delwyn's next attacks. He charged and pushed Delwyn back into the mud. His armor sinking into the ground as the soldier began to force down the wooden shaft over his neck. Delwyn rolled and got on top of the soldier, now choking him. They struggled for a minute until the soldier stopped breathing and went limp. Delwyn then scrambled to find his sword and shield again.

Many others were fighting in the mud, slipping off balance and dragging their enemies down with them. It was hard to tell at some points whose side the soldiers were on. Mud cached their armor and stained their colors. Yet the King's men made themselves known by the direction they fought. Outward from the town walls, they pushed. They resisted any attacker who tried to lay siege to the walled city.

The King and his knights wedged forward through the detachment of soldiers. The city guards pushing behind them. Gusts of wind pulled the rain, slashing down at them. Behind the front line of foot soldiers, mages were waiting for a clear shot at their enemies. As soon as the King could be seen with his men behind him, they went to conjure their fire. Magic left their hands to form a ball of flame. With two hands, the mages threw the fire at the King. Yet once the fire left their hands, it was just fire, no longer being fueled by magic. It steamed and extinguished in the rain. Gabel saw this and went to charge them.

"Even this miserable rain is on our side!" He called. The mages set their hands ablaze and tried to burn the King at close range, but it was no use. Gabel cut across and struck them all down. His bronze sword flashing with the lighting across the sky.

As men fought and died on both sides, the victors were clear. Not one soldier of the Army of the West stepped foot behind the city walls. Eventually the soldiers were driven back and fled into the forest. The city guards and the knights yelling with adrenaline.

"Let it be known today that this land has a King!" Gabel started, the guard raising their weapons and cheering over the thunder. "And that King has not abandoned his people!"

"For the King!" The guards shouted. "For the King! For the King!"

Gabel and his men were taken out of the rain and brought to the city keep. The stone tower lay in the center of the rainy town. Heavy stones held back the thunder rumbling outside. The knights took off their armor and sat by their King next to the roaring hearth. The fire made a small aura of warmth and light in the middle of the dark hall.

"You will be safe here for the night," One of the guardsmen said. His voice echoing through the empty hall. He brought over roasted pork and wine and set it on the table. "Obviously, you are all welcome in Haul as long as you need. We are in your debt for saving us."

"Is there no lord of the keep?" Gabel asked him.

"No," He shook his head. Gabel nodded thoughtfully.

"Thank you," Gabel grabbed a cup of wine. The guard bowed his head then walked back through the dark halls. The King drank his wine and took pieces of the roast to eat.

"Grev will know we're here," said Igran.

"Yes. He will know. But by the time he sends anyone else this way, we'll have an army at our backs."

"Those soldiers came from the capital?" Delwyn asked, whipping the mud off his armor.

"Most likely. There's no major city or stronghold between here and Castle Rock," Gabel answered. He stared into the fire and took in its warmth. It breathed with light and cracked as sparks flew into the air. "You men better rest. We can get supplies here for a few days, but no more. Our way has been perilous thus far. We've been without rest for so long, always leaning into the dangers in our way. Be of good courage, my knights. There will come a day when the rain will end, and we'll all be gathered. The sun will rise on this kingdom again. And that rising will start in the Dawn Mountains. We may have to face struggle awhile longer but know this kingdom will come to salvation."

The Fervent

In the North part of the Avarwood, an old stone hall kept the Fervent Knights out of the rain. Though some of the ceiling had disappeared with time, they were able to find a dry place in the back corner. Cedric tended a fire, glowing off the old stone bricks. Edwards was away from the fire, collecting water that fell steadily off the slope of the caved-in ceiling. Grass grew in patches where the floor used to be, even a tree grew up in the center of this old hall. Stone pillars lay in pieces around them, which the knights used as seats around their fire.

"Explain to us again, Edwards, why we're out here in the rain?" One of the Fervent asked, eating bits from the roast they cooked.

"I told you," The young knight began. "We are among the only ones left in the Realms who still knows the name of our God. I don't know how we have failed so miserably to become such a reclusive order, but we have. I will not stand to let him be forgotten."

"And nor will you if you're faithful to him," Cedric added. "Our brother is right. We've become indolent in our service to Adonai."

"So, what are we to do about it?" Joel, one of the knights, asked. He was a tall man, bald with a bristly grey beard. "We followed the prophets' orders faithfully, for years. And now you're telling me that it wasn't enough? Besides, this isn't exactly the time to travel the world and ask people if they remember their creator."

"No. It is not," Cedric said calmly. "But this is the time when people are without hope and looking for something to set their faith in. The world is enshrouded in great evil and no doubt people have fallen to it because they don't know there is something to have hope in. They don't know there is a God who has set in place a plan to deliver them. They don't know their salvation is riding in with the dawn very soon. Why would we not want to share that news? Such good news of victory. Yes, people believe that their King is alive and will reclaim the throne. But we have all heard the prophecy. It is not this King who will destroy all evil."

"But what are *we* to do?" Joel insisted.

"Pave the way," Edwards said. The fire cracked between them. "We all know the Realms are in turmoil. And though we are not the ones to restore it, we are called to be forces of good. We fight against what evil we face and courageously uphold what is good. All the while, we remain faithful to our King, our God."

"Okay," Another of the Fervent said.

"Thank you, Amos," Cedric said. "Joel?"

"Okay," He nodded and leaned back against the wall and closed his eyes. Edwards sat down next to Cedric and stared into the fire.

"Thank you," The young knight spoke.

"Of course. I know it is hard. There can be lots of doubt. Sometimes this God of ours doesn't seem very tangible. It can hard to know what to do to practically serve him," Cedric sighed. "But in truth he is very present. The fact that he even cares about our world, the trials we face. It brings great hope. He does guard us like a King. We may not see him now… but we fight for his kingdom."

Edwards looked at him, taking in his words.

The next morning, the sun shined through the autumn forest. Leaves were almost all gone at this point. Only the evergreens still looked to be living. Water dripped from the branches and filled between the rocks in the road. As they began riding, they came across a moose, standing on the stone path in front of them. It was tall and could meet the riders in the eye. Its antlers were covered in moss and it snorted vapor in the cool of the morning. The five stopped and sat in silence, unsure of how to proceed. Moose have been known for charging riders in the Avarwood. Once fully grown, they're able to fend off entire hunting parties. It chewed on grass, staring at them between bites. Edwards prompted his horse to take a few steps forward, the horseshoes clicking against the cobblestone. The moose looked up at him with its black eyes. They looked at each other for a moment, then the moose turned its head toward the sky. Edwards looked and saw crows flying overhead.

"Grev," He said aloud. The moose then took a few steps back, out of the road.

"He's letting us through," Amos said.

"Then we mustn't waste time," Cedric kicked his horse and began to ride down the path, the others galloping close behind. The knights rode out of the forest, into the Blackrock Bluffs to the West. The five in white cloaks drove across the rugged landscape, riding along the hills and across shallow rivers. The yellow grass blew in the brisk wind. They followed the crows that flew overhead, riding until they reached a village, nestled in a valley just beside a river. A mill rolled in the running waters. People stopped to see the five white knights on their horses. They looked around but saw no enemies. With that, they proceeded into the village.

"Stay sharp," Cedric said, still scanning the lowly village. People worked quietly outside; their faces kept to the ground. From one of the houses, a woman was crying.

"Please help us," An old woman, covered in dirt clung onto Edwards' cape, still on his horse. Her hands were shaking, and tears were already in her eyes.

"What's happened here?" He leaned down to speak with her.

"The soldiers. They've taken everything. First, they took our men as prisoners. They took Willelm. Then they started to take our food. If we don't produce more for them, they'll kill us all."

"Who's Willelm?" Amos asked.

"Our knight. Willelm the Wanderer. He was the only protection that we had."

"Where are they now?" Cedric asked. The old woman turned and pointed over the hill. In the blank sky, crows circled around.

"There's nothing we can do," Joel whispered to Cedric.

"No, please," The woman turned back to them.

"We will do what we can," Edwards grabbed her hand, trying to calm her down.

"Thank you," She cried. "Thank you."

"When will they come again?" Cedric asked.

"Tomorrow. At dawn."

"Okay," Cedric nodded. The knights left their hoses and gear in an old barn. They walked down to the river, now seeing a bridge further up, passing between the hills. Rapids ran underneath.

"We have to scout out the camp, see how many soldiers we're up against," Cedric said.

"I'll take Harmon," Joel spoke up.

"Very well. Amos and Edwards will stay here and see what fortifications they can make. See if there's any way to hold off an oncoming attack."

"Where are you going?" Amos asked as Cedric was already walking away.

"Going to pray," He called, not looking back. Joel rolled his eyes and left with Harmon.

The two walked up the road and across the bridge to leave town. They could see smoke rising up from behind another hill. Moving up to the top of the ridge, the crawled through the grass and overlooked the soldier camp. A few dozen tents in rows, weapon racks that held swords and spears. A simple wooden tower in the middle, with a lone archer sitting on a stool. The prisoners were kept on the far side of camp, the men tied up to posts by their hands and feet. Among them was a knight in brown and white surcoat. Crows perched on the banners that hung, some left in cages on the ground.

"How many men you think?" Joel asked.

"Maybe fifty," Harmon was still counting in his head. "What are they doing out here? Seems so far from the war."

"I don't know," Joel shook his head and crawled back behind the hill. Harmon took one more looked over the entire camp and then crawled backwards to meet him.

"Anything?" Edwards asked as the two returned.

"Maybe fifty men. A dozen prisoners," Harmon said. "Anything here?"

"The town's open on all sides. Once they get across that bridge, there's no way to defend."

"If we sneak into their camp and free the men, we could have a chance to fight our way out," Amos thought.

"We're still outnumbered two to one, maybe more," Joel shook his head. "We can't attack, and we can't defend. Face it, brothers, this is a lost cause."

"When did you become so defeatist?" Harmon asked.

"No. He's right," Edwards thought.

"I never thought I would hear you say that," Joel folded his arms in satisfaction.

"No, I don't agree we should give up," Edwards shook his head. "We don't have enough men to attack and we don't have enough here to defend from an attack. We need to split them up."

"How?" Amos asked.

"Tomorrow they come to collect the food. I doubt they would send everyone. We need to hit them when their forces are dived. *Then*, we might have a chance to save this town."

"But we still wouldn't have enough men here to stop them from coming," Harmon said. Edwards thought for a moment. Looking out, he saw Cedric crossing the high bridge to get back into the village.

"Maybe we don't have to."

The knights worked the rest of that day to make preparations in town. They gathered what tools and rope they could find, not resting until the sun went down. Edwards was up practicing with his sword, dueling his shadow in the streets. Cedric heard him from the stables and went out to meet him.

"I know the others may doubt," Cedric began. "But I know we are doing the right thing."

"Maybe. I have a hard time ignoring Joel," Edwards sheathed his sword. "What if he's right? What if this is just a lost cause?"

"You are a knight of the Fervent order. You fight for one cause, and it is never *lost*. If we perish, we perish. But the cause is no less good. To die in battle is honorable, sure. But to lay down your life for another, for a stranger? To follow what you know is right. There is no greater glory among men."

"Thank you, Cedric."

"Do not lose hope," The old knight put his hand on Edwards' shoulder.

As dawn came up over the bluffs, all was quiet. No villager was outside, only the pigs and cattle, fenced in their pens. Across the hills, a band of Grev's soldiers began along the road, following a single horse, pulling an empty cart. They were dressed in chainmail and violet sashes. They walked out of their camp and up the road toward the village to collect their demanded food supply. After camp was behind them, two men in white cloaks moved across the ridge overlooking camp. The archer on his stool sat and stared blankly, not expecting any sort of trouble this far from conflict.

Joel and Harmon moved down the hill and hid themselves behind the prisoners. Men young and old were all tied, helpless. The white knights peered between the posts to see if they were being watched.

"Okay, listen up," Joel started. "Once we cut you loose, you run for the weapons rack. Got it?" They saw the prisoners nod their heads without speaking.

"Willelm, can you lead these men?" Harmon asked.

"Certainly," The wandering knight said, looking forward. He was middle aged, brown hair and beard.

Joel and Harmon then went behind each of the posts and cut the binds around their hands and feet. As soon as they were free, the men rushed to wooden racks of swords and spears.

"Hey!" One of the soldiers yelled when he spotted them. The prisoners took no time cutting down the soldiers that came out of their tents. Most of them unarmed and without any protection. The archer stood up once he noticed what was happening. He fired down on them, taking his time between shots. One prisoner was shot in the chest, his sword falling from his hand. An enemy soldier quickly picked it up and began fighting off the attack.

Soldiers at the other end of camp armed themselves and rushed to meet the battle. The archer fired straight down on the men, the arrows piercing the ground at their feet. Eventually, the prisoners began to push the rickety wooden tower. The archer dropped to the platform in fear when he felt it move. It rocked and came out of the ground, falling backwards onto the row of tents.

"Back to the West with ya!" Willelm took the spears like javelins and threw them at the far-off soldiers. He struck down several before arming himself with a sword to engage close quarters.

"What in the blazes is going on out there?" An officer yelled form inside the head tent.

"Nevermind that! You need to get this letter to Castle Rock. The King has been spotted at Haul. We need reinforcements at once!"

Then one of the officers ran out of the tent as he stuffed a letter into his uniform. Joel and Harmon exchanged looks and pushed forward to get to him. The officer ran to get to his horse, dodging the battle all around him.

"Willelm!" Harmon pointed. The knight grabbed a spear from the ground and threw it at him. It cut through the officer's leg, pinning him to the ground. The officer stopped one of his soldiers running by.

"Take this letter to Grev! Go!" He handed it off to the soldier before the knights could reach him. The soldier ran to the nearest horse. Willelm was going for another spear but was attacked from the side. He use the spear handle to block, then dropped it in exchange for his sword. He glanced to see the soldier on the horse taking off down the road.

Across the hills, the line of soldiers marched on, oblivious to what was happening behind them. They saw the village in front of them, just across the river. One of the soldiers stopped as he overlooked the town.

"What is it?" The man driving the cart asked. He remained silent for a moment, not seeing anyone around. From behind the watermill, the soldier thought he saw someone in white, but they vanished.

"It's nothing. Let's keep moving," He said, and they began across the high bridge. Once the band of soldiers were all on the bridge, Edwards came out from behind the mill.

"What's that?" A soldier asked as Edwards took a rope from the ground and hooked it to the water wheel. The wheel pulled on the roped and began to wrap it around itself. The rope tightened and the soldiers followed it to find the other end was tied to the supports of the bridge.

"Shit," They scrambled to get off, but it was too late. The wheel pulled out the support beams and the bridge collapsed. The soldiers and the cart fell with it. They fell down the cliff and crashed into the rapids.

Those soldiers who made it across looked on in horror as their comrades, and their way back, were gone. Cedric, Edwards, and Amos came out from the village with their swords in hand. The soldiers rushed to meet them. Edwards skillfully exchanged blows with the soldiers, blocking with his sword and delivering attacks in return.

Amos was backing up down the hill as two soldiers charged at him. He warded them off, continuing to walk backwards as he did so. Amos was smaller than the soldiers who slashed at him, barley keeping his sword up to defend himself. He tripped and fell down the incline. One of the soldiers swung down to kill him, but Cedric stuck his sword out to block. The other soldier took advantage of his exposed side and cut him down.

"No!" Edwards screamed and left the opponent he was dueling to tackle the soldier that had just killed Cedric. They went tumbling down the hill, each striking the other as they rolled. When they reached the bottom, the soldier struck his head against a rock and fell dead.

Amos got to his feet and engaged the other soldier. Soon, Amos was again backing up as he was being attacked. His feet ever inching toward the cliffside, with the river far below. The soldier noticed this and lunged out with his sword to push Amos off, but he stepped to the side and pulled the soldier over the cliff instead. He fell into the water and was quickly picked up by the current.

Harmon and Joel led the charge out of camp right behind Sir Willelm. And the surviving prisoners behind them. In the wreckage of camp, the last officer pulled the bow from the dead archer and took aim. He fired at the men running up the hill and struck Harmon in the back. Joel was running away too fast to even notice.

As they got to the collapsed bridge, they saw the soldier on his horse, looking down onto the scene. He turned when he heard the men running up behind him.

"Wait," He put his hands up, the letter still clenched in his fist. Joel and Willelm pointed their swords at him. "Now just wait."

"Hand over that letter," Joel said.

"Okay," The soldier held it out. Joel approached slowly, then took it from his hand.

"You know what it said?" Joel asked.

"No. I swear."

"Okay. Go," He waved the soldier away, who kicked his horse and rode off along the river. They caught their breath for a moment and saw that the fight had ended on the other side of the river.

"Can you guys get across?" Amos called over to them.

"We'll take the long way around," One of the prisoners responded.

"Is that Cedric?" Joel asked, seeing Edwards kneeling next to the old knight. Amos nodded.

"And Harmon?" Amos called from across the river. Only then did Joel realize he was not with them.

"Dammit," Joel shook his head. He glared over at Edwards.

The prisoners went down the hill and crossed the river at its shallow point. The women of the town came out from their houses to see the men crossing the river. They cried with joy to see their sons and husbands returned to them. Joel went straight for Edwards, burning with rage until he saw Sir Willelm coming up to him.

"Thank you," He said to Joel.

"Of course," Joel tried to move passed him.

"What lord do you men serve?"

"What?" He stopped.

"What lord sent you? I haven't seen any other knights between here and the Lake Realm."

"We serve our God, Adonai. He is our lord," He replied, still confused.

"You sure you're not mercenaries that were hired to attack those men?"

"No. We serve only our God and do what is right."

"Then surely he has sent you to us. This God of yours saw us in our misery and sent you," He said.

"He... he has," Joel thought. The people of the town continued to revel in their victory. Tears of joy and mourning all fed into the buzz of the village that day.

"I'm sorry," Joel went up to Edwards later as they were packing in the barn. The horses already prepared to set out again.

"What?"

"I am sorry," Joel said again. "You were right. I think this was the right thing. That knight, Willelm, was asking me questions about Adonai all afternoon. He couldn't believe that we weren't paid by a lord to rescue them."

"This is how it spreads," Edwards nodded. "I think this is how people will know about their God."

"Through battle?"

"Not necessarily, but through the things we do. Acts of good. Acts of love. That knight will go and tell others how Adonai saved him from peril."

"Maybe so," Joel thought. "I will follow you in this. If this is something Cedric was willing to die for, it must've been the right thing."

"We both know that old man wouldn't die for anything else. Thank you, Joel."

"Of course."

The Chief

The King and his knights went down to the docks in the city of Haul. Longships were moored to the wooden piers just outside the walls. The men in their cloaks walked down to the docks as waves crashed into the rocky shore. White water sprayed into the air with each rushing wave. One of the longships was preparing to go underway. A sailor next to the ship waved over to the knights.

"Your highness," The sailor greeted.

"We were told this could take us to the other side of the bay?" Gabel asked.

"Aye, sir. We'll row you to Lake Shore. The village is at the foot of the mountains. From there you can take the pass to Oorog."

"Thank you, sailor."

Gabel and his knights loaded themselves onto the longship. Soon, the ship was filled with men who were sitting along either side. Each had a long oar dipping in the water. The ship was cast off from its moorings and the men began to row at the beat of a kettle drum. With each pound, the captain would shout "Row!" The sailors pulled back on their oars and began to push the ship into the choppy waves. Sailors unfurled the single sail and tied down its lines. Gusts off the bay filled the sail propelled them further through the water. The bow of the longship rose up from the keel and was carved to look like the head of a serpent. The stern was carved and sharped to look like its tail.

The winds and jagged rocks of the Lake Realm made seafaring difficult, but this crew of sailors were well used to the late season gales. Waves pounded rhythmically against the haul of the ship, keeping in time with the rowers. Fog lifted to reveal steep fjords and stacks. They were like great spears against the cliffsides, jutting out from the waters as the roots of the mountains dove deep below the surface. Lining the north shore of this great bay were the Dawn Mountains. The snowcaps reached the heavens, scraping the clouds that floated by.

The town of Lake Shore was wedged between two of these cliffs faces, on a stretch of low-level shoreline. A small canyon created the trail up from the town. The longship furled its sail as they rowed into the dock. Sailors threw over the mooring lines and worked to secure their oars.

"Hail the King," The sea captain saluted as the three left the ship and went up into the town. Lake Shore was nothing but tiny village in the small stretch. Fisherman and sailors built houses here and occasionally traded with the orcs up the mountains.

The canyon leading out of town was narrow with steep cliffs built up on either side. There was no green plant life.

Only hard rock. The trail was rough, often winding up seemingly vertical faces. The path now scaled the side of the stone wall, on top of the deep chasm. It led the men to a narrow cave. They pulled themselves up the rock and into the tunnel that went through the mountain side, reappearing shortly after its entrance. After emerging from the cave, the men continued to climb higher in elevation. The slate rock was brittle in some parts, breaking and sliding from under their feet. The intense hike was balanced by the cool of the morning and the fog that dampened the dark stone. Delwyn and Igran especially slowed by their armor.

By now, the men could see the vast expanse of the Orcish Realm. The mountain territory fit the hardiness of its people, the orcs. Snow covered peaks accented the land of dark rock. Oorog, the orc's capital was more or less the orcs biggest war camp. Huts and long houses were built high on the level ground that the mountains offered, next to a spring of fresh water. Wooden palisades marked their city borders along with sharp cliffs. The men were met by a host of Orcish guards upon arrival.

"Halt! What business do you have here, humans?" The orc was tall, built like a bull, and had an ashen color to his skin, as did most orcs. His leather armor was lined with furs to keep warm in the cooler climate.

King Gabel removed his hood and showed his face to the guard. "I am one who you know. I am Gabel, High King of the Realms," The orc guards bent their knees to the King.

"My liege. It is an honor to welcome you into our city. Our chief will want to hear of your arrival," The guards went back to their post and the one orc escorted the men through the rocky roads of Oorog. From inside the city walls, one could see mountains in every direction. The King dropped back to Igran.

"Mind you keep your tongue. We are here to make peace; not start another war. I understand their chief is still Orubark and I shouldn't have to remind you to set aside your temper."

"Yes sir," Igran said.

They proceeded to the great longhouse which stood tallest amongst the buildings. In the longhouse, Orubark was behind a set of maps, several of his officers were also discussing with him. They spoke of current battles and warring raids with goblins. The vicious beings also dwelled in these mountains and the dark forests to the North. They lived in packs and attacked Orcish villages in large swarms. The orcs and the goblins have their war seasons in the colder months when resources become scarcer. The two civilizations, if one could call goblins civilized, would compete for food, raiding from each other.

"My King!" Orubark welcomed as he saw the men enter. "It has been too long."

"Chief Orubark," Gabel greeted.

"I assume you didn't trek out here to enjoy the view. Although, I believe it is worth the hike," The older orc spoke in a low tone.

"Afraid not, in fact I should assume you know why it is I am here," Gabel replied to the leader of the orcs.

"Ah. I should have known. I heard the rumors that the throne was overtaken and that you however were missing and, yet still alive. I didn't know what to make of it, but couriers and scouts eventually brought back enough info to the clan. Yes, I know why you have come, to use the King's secret army. Am I correct?" Orubark asked Gabel from across the table.

"You will not be the only. An army of men has risen, without my influence."

"Without your influence? My King, if your loyal people has risen to the occasion to fight and reclaim the throne in your glory, that has been done by your good influence."

"Perhaps so. And yes, I have come here because in my Realm the men have fallen. Greed and cowardice have cracked humanity and now there is nowhere safe. I come to you, to call upon you and your army."

"I am honored to say the least, that you have thought of us after so many years. Alas, we are entering our war season. I'm afraid we must keep what troops we have to ward off the goblins for the winter."

"Your war seasons. What luxury is it that you choose when and when not to enter a war. A threat has taken this kingdom and good people in every realm will die if we do not push back, yours included. The bloody goblins will come and go with the seasons. You hit them this year, they'll be back the next. The whole Realms is in grave danger, Chief. I would not have called for your aid if you did not lead the best army these Realms had witnessed. Yes, I could mention the pact that Castle Rock has with the orcs. That since we do not wield an army, you are to step in if the time needs it."

The King sighed then continued. "But I should hope that your cause to fight this is not because you ought to. There is a ruler in that castle that threatens everyone's way of life, and it is our responsibility to take it back. And not for our glory, but for those who have none. For the people. I came asking because it is only in your nature to answer. To be the army of good when evil rises."

"What you speak is true. My liege, I shall assemble my troops. Let it be known that there will be a day where you sit in that fancy throne of yours again, even if I must carry you to it!" Orubark went from his desk and entered the main hall. "Gather the troops. Let them know we are marching south," He said to one of his officers.

"To where, Chief?"

"To Castle Rock."

Outside the walls of the long house, companies of orcs began to form. They were quick to answer their orders. Each soldier with uniformed metal armor, insulated with furs. They each carried a reinforced wooden shield and a sword. The old shields had their family's coat of arms, painted with different colors and symbols. The high forges were burning with new weapons to make. Delwyn and Igran went to the blacksmith, who worked mechanically to pour steel into molds.

"Excuse me," Delwyn said. "We were told you could fashion us new armor," The orc looked at the knights' broken chainmail and split up cuirasses. "The King also requires a suit; he is without any."

"Just leave the old one's here," The smith grunted then went back to pouring molten metal.

Orubark and Gabel stood on the steps of the longhouse, looking out over the mountains, each holding a cup of wine.

"It is a new age, Gabel. In all of our loses, perhaps this has renewed our spirit and will remind the world of this kingdom's strength."

"Aye this is the dawn of a new age, but we must first fight out of the night. But I have gone to thinking, maybe the kingdom could use a change."

"What do you mean?"

"I will not be ruler forever. When I am gone, the people will need a guiding light."

"I don't understand. You have your son as heir."

"Yes, but who will my son be? I have been called more righteous than any other King. But I will be remembered as Gabel the Strong, slayer of beasts. When we take the kingdom back, I do not want it to be the same as it was. Red and Gold. Valor, honor, and wisdom. It was not over these things that the war started. It was not these that my kingdom really stands for. But righteousness, purity, goodness. It is these things I want our people to fight for. It is these I hope to be remembered for."

"Then let it be so, my King."

Orubark went to the orcs and had them paint over their shields. Their many crests were all covered with a solid grey. Then in the center, in snow white was painted a slightly different coat of arms. It was a shattered crown with a sword piercing through it and the angel wings coming out from that.

Everyone was gathered in the longhouse that night. A great feast was custom to the orcs before marching to war. They had roasted lamb and fresh breads. They drank mead and wines; everyone ate to their heart's content. Gabel stood near the end of the meal and raised his cup. The rows of feasting orcs stopped and gave him their attention.

"The Greyland Realms. The finest kingdom to have ever graced this land. A kingdom established by God for all people. Now, Grev wants to throw that all away and rule with tyranny. He wants to destroy our peace and defile what is good. If Grev wants change, then he'll get it. He thinks he can push this kingdom down, but we will come back stronger than before. We bear new colors, we wield new knights, and a have new fire in our hearts! The first King of these Realms, King Greyland, brought each people together under one pact, uniting the Realms through peace, walking beside our God, pursuing what is right and just. Let us not forget where we have started and let us not lose sight of where we are to go," Gabel took one of the new shields and held it in front of the crowd.

"Each of you, have faith in what will come, a better kingdom. We must become better, not for ourselves, but because the people of this land need us to be. We must reestablish ourselves in our knightlihood. Realign ourselves to the principles this kingdom was founded on. In honor of King Greyland, let us change our colors to his and we affirm ourselves as the Greyland Knights!" The King raised his glass as his men and the orc officers applauded.

"Igran, Delwyn, Orubark, would you kneel?" The King took a sword and walked over to them. The three kneeling on the stone floor in front of him. "Under your sacred honor, do you reaffirm your allegiance to this kingdom, to the Greyland Realms?"

"Yes, sire," Delwyn answered. Igran and Orubark both nodding with and replying "Yes."

"Do you vow to uphold, to fight, and protect the rules of law, to pursue righteousness, and to keep the highest chivalry among people?"

"Yes," They answered. Gabel approached his knights and with the sword, tapped them on each shoulder.

"My knights, rise. I award you each a grey cloak to cover your armor. So, you may clothe yourselves with what is just and pure. And to each of you, I give a silver ring with the new crest our kingdom. The broken crown to say that kingdoms will rise and fall, but also the sword. So, you may know that the God who walked with Greyland, will fight for you always. These would serve as signs of your knightlihood."

The knights stood and took the cloaks and put on the signet rings. The army behind them applauded again. Igran put his hand on Delwyn's shoulder and chuckled, the younger knight smiling. Everyone burning with joy and hope.

"My King…" Orubark began. "It would not be right if only we were to receive such gifts," He motioned over to the smith who brought over an object concealed in a scarlet cloth. Gabel studied its round shape for a moment. Then he pulled off the cloth to reveal a crown casted in gold. The points were square, like the ramparts of a watchtower. "I know it is not the same, but the world should know that we are marching behind a King."

Gabel looked at it thoughtfully before picking it up and placing it on his greying red hair.

"Long live the King!" Orubark announced.

"Long live the King!" The chorus followed. "Long live the King! Long live the King!"

After dinner passed, the men and the Orcs struck conversation with each other. Igran, though in high spirit, sat by himself at the table where they had previously feasted. He slowly finished his cup of wine, taking in the mountain view out the window. Orubark saw and went over to him.

"Sir Igran, am I correct?" The orc asked him. He nodded.

"Sir Orubark now, has a decent ring to it," Igran turned to the orc who had now sat next to him.

"I wanted to address something with you-"

"No bother," Igran put up his hand. "That time has passed."

"That it has. And you know her death was not of my own doing. Citizens on both sides were lost in that crossfire so many years ago."

"I am aware. And now, only now have I seen that. Traveling here, I was sure I was going to lose my temper with your people for I had known them cruel. Alas, I have learned otherwise. Your men, this army, snapped together without question. They bravely live out their lives as warriors and while they could have stayed and fought here, they had no issue with fighting our war."

"As your King said, this is *everyone's* war. I am glad to hear you no longer think us savages," Igran nodded, they shook hands and parted. Gabel had witnessed the interaction and slightly raised his glass at Igran.

Delwyn was standing outside, unnoticed, holding onto his old blue cape. The color of Thundertree yet was now battered and torn. He held onto it for a moment, remembering where the cape was from, then he let it blow away on the mountain wind. He watched it disappear and with it, let go of his old life.

The men prepped themselves that night, gathering their supplies and packing all they would need for the long march south. For at dawn, they would leave for war.

The Warrior

Saint George's men were gathered inside the walls. The mead hall overflowed and soldiers broke bread with each other in their tents. Everyone huddling together as they have been over the past weeks. They played on pipes and fiddles, playing old songs from old wars. Their lyrics rang with new meaning. The word of war now meant something tangible to these men. It was no longer history, but very preset. From a private room in the guildhall, the knights met to dine with themselves and discuss the plans of attack.

"I reckon we have close to nine hundred men by this point," Adir looked out the tall narrow windows at the large crowds of soldiers. Many were camped outside the city walls in tents and huts that peppered the once lonesome slopes of Saint George.

"Aye," Sven handed him a cup of wine. "And what are we to do with all these men?" He turned to the prince.

"I am no leader of armies, but I would say we should leave in the morning," The young man said nobly.

"Tomorrow? We have no word yet from Igran or the King. Should we not wait for their orders?" Ragnar asked.

"No," Sven added. "We have to take the fort soon. Yes, we must wait to siege the castle, but we cannot wait any longer to take the fort. I agree with the prince, let us march on in the morrow, while the men are anxious and ready. We should wait no more days. Winter is quickly approaching and then we would have a huge disadvantage. We must go now," Sven shook his head.

"Let us go," Adir said.

"Very well," Ragnar sighed and got up to leave.

"Where are you going?" Adir caught him.

"If we're leaving tomorrow, I have preparations to make. You know how ceremonial us northerners are," He chuckled as he left. The others remained and listened to the chatter outside and took in the music being played.

What purpose were we called?
For what cause shall we fall,
That we are to fight under standard?
Stand together in the nigh
March forth in the day
Fight onward as men who've been banded.

O onward we go, men. Onward we go
I'll grab the sword and you'll aim the bow
And to our glory death, we yell ev'n so
Onward we go, men. Onward we go

Our flesh just as scarred,
But what steel matches ours,
If we fight for King and for homeland?

Stand with me now
And do not low'r your brow
Fight onward for that bright land!

O onward we go, men. Onward we go
I'll grab the sword and you'll aim the bow
And to our glory death, we yell ev'n so
Onward we go, men. Onward we go

Though we may pass away
Though our bodies see decay
We press on toward the morrow
Tis there that we fight
And there we may die
Fight onward as men of no sorrows.

O onward we go, men. Onward we go.
I'll grab the sword and you'll aim the bow
And to our glory death, we yell ev'n so
Onward we go, men. Onward we go

"Lord Sven," Ivan spoke up.

"Yes, my liege?"

"Find that young smith some armor. The one I dueled in the yard. He doesn't have any. I assure he's among the best fighters we have. He'll need it."

"Yes sir," Sven nodded and left.

The next morning, Saint George woke to sounds of strife. Word had gone out that they would take the fort. Men were quickly making their final preparations before going out into warfare. They packed their swords and strung their bows. The smith's forge had been glowing hot for many a day now and would not cease as long as there were weapons to be made. The patchwork band of farmers and guildsmen were now well put as an army.

Troops garrisoned outside of the town's walls. Men armed themselves and moved into ranks. Swords and shields at the ready. Hundred flooded out of the town. Few souls still remained within the town walls, only women, children, or any elderly man who could no longer fight. The Prince sat outside his tent and was putting on his suit of black armor.

"Appreciate the gift, your lordship," Myles called as he walked over. He wore a fine chainmail shirt with shoulder plates secured with leather straps. He also had been given grieves for his legs and bracers for his arms. Dawnsmist, the King's sword, he wore on a belt around his waist.

"I'm starting to think the titles you give are ingenuine."

"Never," Myles put his hand on his chest to act offended.

"Are you ready?" Ivan asked him.

"I sure hope so. Happening into a fight is different from marching out to meet one. Are you?"

"We'll see. I've never been in a battle before. Can't say I've lived enough to see one before today. My father lived through many great battles. All the Kings have."

"Then certainly, you are ready. As heir to the kingdom, you've been bred for this. Consider their strength in you."

They heard Sven across camp giving orders to men as they were preparing to leave.

"Go scout out the fort. Let us know what we're up against," Sven ordered a group of men. "Rest of you, form ranks! Adir, get your brother and pick a battalion to march with!"

"I haven't seen him since last night, but I'll let him know," Adir replied.

Myles turned back to Ivan.

"Come on then, we shouldn't keep the war waiting."

Down the road, Ragnar was riding his horse at a sprint. Its horseshoes clipped the rocky ground. He rode through the highlands, heading westward. He rode through the mist of the morning until he came to a lowly farmstead. He stepped off from his horse and went toward the wooden fence. Alessia came to the road for she heard the horse approaching.

"Do you not have a battle, Sir Ragnar? Or have you come back to tell me how the war is going?" She asked lightly.

"Alessia, would you ride into battle with me?" Ragnar grabbed her hands.

"What?"

"I could fight in this world alone, but I don't want to. Will you fight with me?"

"Surely, yes," She said before even thinking. "But won't this take away from your glory? Asking a woman to fight by your side?"

"To hell with glory. You're the best fighter we've got. We need you. I need you."

"Aye. I'll get my sword."

Alessia sat on the saddle behind Ragnar as he whipped the horse to start again down the road. She held onto his sides as they galloped toward the marching army of Saint George.

"What news do you bring?" Sven called, who trotted his horse to meet the scouts returning to the army.

"Fort Redmont's expecting for us, my lord. They have archers, by the hundreds locked behind those walls. Yet the way is clear."

"Then by all means, let's walk right up to the bastards!" Sven turned his horse around. "Onward!" The army marched forth with the constant clank of metal keeping their rhythmic pace. Miles they would march along the road, down the highlands and into the dense pines.

As dusk appeared, the sounds of the approaching army could be heard by the archers on the other side of a stone wall. The men who had been obediently standing out in the cold now readied their bows and passed their commands to each other by whisper.

Sven walked his army only paces away from the forts gate. The large wooden doors were shut and barred. No guard was standing on the wall. No torches to light Fort Redmont. All was dark and silent.

"Are you sure there's another army in there? There is no sign of any enemy," Sven turned to his scouts.

"They are all inside the walls, standing like stone."

"Very well. Ready your swords!" Sven shouted over his army. Hundreds of men unsheathed their weapon.

"Look sir!" A young soldier pointed to the night sky. A dark mass seemed to be moving upward against the darkening sky. The cloud shot up and then came back down. A single arrow then landed at the feet of Sven's horse.

"Shields!" Sven ordered in a great panic. But one after the other, arrows fell on the men. Many striking into the exposed skin of the soldiers or glancing off of their armor. They all broke rank and dove for cover or hid under their shields. They scurried around as the hail of arrows dropped on their heads. Some of the men dropped their torches, which started little fires, lighting up the battleground. In the chaos, the town's gates open and flooded out it's foot soldiers.

Men with swords and spears charged the attacking army, still struggling to their feet. Violet banners and ribbons roared in the rush of the men who carried them. Their ranks cut through Saint George, but they were not without fight. The men leapt to their feet; their swords ready to meet their foes. Sven fell off his horse, but scrabbled to attack his enemies.

"Push back!" He yelled to his men. "Fight back!" His men did so, but not with ease. They continued to bring their ranks closer to the front lines nearing the gate. A faint cry for archers brought forth another hail of arrows down on the men. Adir the Mighty was struck in the shoulder and collapsed off his horse. He fell to the cold, dark ground.

He was lost among the many men, battling for their lives. He crawled forward toward the nearest enemy soldier, he sprung up from the earth and brought the soldier down into a struggle. They wrestled in the dirt, Adir having the upper hand, took a spear that lay close and stabbed his foe. He looked around but could not see his brother.

"Ragnar, where are you?" He said between his teeth. As he got up to fight another soldier.

"Dammit! They started without us!" Ragnar shouted as he rode into the battle. With his hammer, he hacked at those who came toward them. His horse kicked and bit at the men who stabbed it. Alessia drew her sword and jumped off the horse. She swung the sword around and slashed down at soldiers who came at them. Ragnar also leaped from the horse and plowed over enemies with his warhammer. The two fought side by side, often both attacking the same opponent.

"Would you care for the shield, m'lady?" Ragnar hollered over as he had it raised to block a barrage of attacks.

"You're too kind," She laughed as she struck down yet another foe. "But I think you need it more than I."

Myles fought with a sword that reflected the moon. He parried and counted quickly, taking no time between opponents. He blocked incoming attacks from multiple soldiers, giving him no opportunity to attack.

"Ivan, I need a hand!" He yelled heard no answer. Myles pushed one of the soldiers back and stabbed the other. Looking around, he couldn't find his comrade.

Ragnar looked up to see a great warrior appear from the town's gates. His silhouette, burning against fires from within the fortress, casted a shadow over the fight. A man of giant stature holding two flails in his right hand. And a round shield in his left. The dark eyes behind the sallet helm scanned the battle.

"Adir!" Ragnar called for his brother. He saw him hacking down soldiers with an axe and sword. "Adir!" The elder brother turned and looked where Ragnar was pointing. Bramus the Conqueror had entered the battlefield. Adir pointed his sword at Bramus from across the fight. The lord saw his challenger.

"You're dead!" He called from beneath his beard. Bramus plowed through the fight, clearing the way with the ball and chains. Adir chopped down on Bramus' shield with his axe. But the collision with his opponent threw him back. Adir rolled to the side as flails impacted the ground. Bramus pulled his weapons up and swung them over his head before lashing out. Adir dodged again and rammed himself into Bramus' shield. Adir pushed his opponent back a few steps. Bramus swung his weapons, but the flails reached around the shield and struck him in the arm. Bramus screaming in pain. The chains only clashing with the back of Adir's cuirass. Adir pulled his axe from the shield and went to slash down. Bramus brought his flails up and across, hitting the knight in the chest and sending him flying back.

"Brother!" Ragnar let out.

Adir pushed himself off his back, his ribs broken beneath his armor. Bramus took a spear from a fallen soldier. The lord threw it like a javelin, the blade driving into Adir's stomach

"No!" Ragnar screamed. He filled with rage and dashed through the mess of the battle, charging at the Bramus. Ragnar shoved others haphazardly out of his way and went to avenge his brother. He tackled the lord from his blindside and brought him fiercely to the ground. Ragnar beat him with violence and wrath. With his bare hands, he ripped Bramus' helmet off and caved the man's face in with continuous blows. He stopped when he realized Bramus has dead. The raging sweat dripped off of Ragnar's brow as he caught his breath. He then scrambled over to his brother.

"Adir. Adir, I'm here."

"Brother," Adir coughed up blood.

"You got this. You're Adir the Mighty. You can make it. You can get through this"

"No. No... Ragnar the Mighty," Adir said. Ragnar shook his head a cried, holding his brother. "Be strong, little brother."

Yet the fight was still roaring, and no one took notice of this. The men of Saint George pushed the fort's forces back into the town. They ran over a great deal of bodies on their way in. The corpses were covered in blood and dirt, so much that it was difficult to distinguish between which side they fought for. Sven remained in the ranks of soldiers, fighting his way forward.

Once the flood of his men was upon the town, it was impossible to stop. One of the guards was trying to close the gate, but there were too many men crossing. Men clashed in the streets, the sharp steel piercing through the plates and links of each other's armor. Archers from the ramparts of the town fired down into the river of charging men. The men of Saint George fought their way further into the town, taking out the archers and seeking soldiers who were now in hiding. Villagers hid in their houses if they couldn't escape into the woods.

As dawn came over the walls, the struggle was dying out. Yet, from his hall, staggered Captain Ballard. He limped with his face dripping with sweat and his sword dropping blots of blood. Sven went ahead of his men, to take this man for himself. The two circled each other, staring the other down with a look of hatred.

"Traitor," Sven said.

Ballard spat at the ground where his enemy paced. He then, striked first. The swords of the two men crashed together. Ballard's moments were quick and of haste, but Sven countered them and landed his own attacks. Back and forth they went. They struck with anger and spite for one another. Meanwhile, the rest of the town was being secured by the peasant army of Saint George. Sven lanced toward his foe, slicing at Ballard's forearm. To which, in pain he dropped his sword. The steel craft fell hard to the dirt.

"You are no more than dung to this kingdom," Sven raved at Ballard who was gripping his torn arm. "You captain have betrayed your people. You are wanted no more," Sven quickly flicked his sword. Cutting his check, Ballard fell to the ground. He reached for his blade, but Sven's foot crushed Ballard's fingers that nearly touched the hilt.

The captain screamed in more pain. Sven's sword was raised overhead. With a single motion, the blade cut through Ballard's neck. Decapitating him in one slice. Sven kicked his enemy's sword and walked away, regaining his breath. Some of his soldiers quickly brought their focus to the main gate. Ragnar walked over the bodies and the blood, carrying his brother, Adir, in his arms. He moved slowly, making his way to Sven.

"How could this be?"

"Your silver tongue led all these men to die," Ragnar spoke. "You talked them up and assured them a swift victory," Many soldiers that lay about wounded and scarred now listened in. "My brother died a warrior's death, but he did it following you. He, like all of us followed you," Ragnar was still in tears. "You had no tactic. That thought of glory tainted your thinking. Have you done this for your King or for your own image? Never have I seen a commander waltz so blindly into battle."

"Do not be distasteful of our victory because of the loss of your brother. Many brothers died here, this day. You have known from the start that I am no military commander, but I was the one who stepped into that role because that's exactly what the people needed. They needed a leader in a time when the throne is broken," Sven sighed. "I morn for him now, just as you do. Adir was my friend as well." Sven looked up to see Alessia, whom he did not know, sobbing at the sight. "We all make sacrifices in war."

That night the men prepared a ceremony for Adir and all the men who had fallen in the Battle of Fort Redmont. They made pyres and burned the men's bodies and sent their ashes to the heavens. In death, these fighters were equal. Ragnar stared at the flams for hours as the pyres burned up. He was out of his armor at this point, wearing just his tunic.

"Ragnar," Alessia locked arms with him and held his hand. "Will you get rest?"

The knight nodded and followed Alessia's lead to a sheltered alley. The survivors camped right on the streets, on straw and crates. Taking whatever rest they could find. The two sat on the ground, Alessia leaning against him and Ragnar holding her from behind. Her long amber hair blazed in the torchlight. They kept close until they drifted to sleep.

Before dawn when the crickets had just begun to chirp, Ivan stepped out the wooden gate and went onto the road. Sven caught sight of this and went up to him outside of the fort's walls.

"Why do you run, my prince?"

"I am not my father's son. I am a coward; I did not fight today. I only lifted my shield in fear, yet I was in no range of the enemy."

"That may be so, but now isn't the time to back down. We have all made mistakes, no one of those men is *all* honorable. Now, in the break of war, we mustn't fumble over our past. Mustn't let our vices hinder us. Right now, is the time to move forward, be better than who you were yesterday."

"Yesterday I stood behind the safety of the army. Yesterday I believed that Grev was justified. Yesterday I abandoned my sister. I am undoubtedly the Shameful Prince! A black sheep in the lineage of great men. No father, not mine, would want a son of me."

"You know your faults, but do not let them eat you. We must move forward. Be better, if not for your sister, your father, then be better for you. Make yourself the hero in your own eyes. I beg you, do not go," Sven spoke soft to the young prince. "There is still a chance for redemption."

"I'm just a boy, youngest among any of these men and I do not have the gut to fight. I know my father is alive and I don't dare face him, not with all I've done."

"You may not fight, whether you wield a weapon or not is your choice, my prince. I am asking you to stay.

Only then, would the opportunity for redemption be available," Ivan swallowed back his emotion and nodded.

The Army

Far to the North, in the Dawn Mountains, an army dressed in grey marched down the pass. They flew their banners and stepped in perfect, disciplined unison. The King led the company of orcs, riding on horseback. Now he wore a suit of steel armor, no longer left to fight in his royal garments. His knights were also mounted on horses and walked behind him. The march out of the mountains was slow, the battalions having to walk in lines of three on the narrow cliff sides. They weaved through passes and around peaks and valleys. The army stretched on for miles.

The thousands made their way to the foothills, marching past farms and old watchtowers. Most villages this far north were small and had no guards to even question the campaign. The foothills rippled out into the Blackrock Bluffs, badlands to the north of the Royal Plains. Horned bison occupied much of the land, grazing in the valleys below the rocky hills. Patches of forest were few and far between. The road through the Bluffs was just as rugged. It rolled over hills and around the large black boulders.

The hardy orcs never stopped to rest during the day. They simply marched on under the standards of the King that flew above them. They would be uncontested the whole way except for a small encampment west of the city of Haul.

"Prepare to attack," Igran rode his horse back through the lines of soldiers. The orcs took their shields off their backs and drew their swords.

"Form ranks!" Orubark ordered as he took out two hand axes. Between the army and this small camp was a herd of bison passing the road. The large animals snorted and huffed as they crossed through the valley.

"Get up!" A spearman called down from atop a lone wooden watchtower. "The army's here!" Men below got out of their tents and quickly threw on armor and found their swords. Only about forty men were left from the assault on Haul. "It's the King!" He shouted down again when he saw Gabel's sword reflecting at them.

"Where are our reinforcements?" One of Grev's soldiers asked aloud.

"None came," His officer replied. "Brace yourselves!" He called to the soldiers.

A few hundred yards away, the King on his horse circled in front of his soldiers.

"If these rebels are the only resistance we meet, then Grev was a fool to underestimate us," He said. "Ready yourselves."

The hundreds of bison between the two began to pick up speed as they crossed over the road. Soldiers on either side were anxiously waiting for the way to clear, leaning forward, and tapping the hilts of their weapons. The horned beasts charged into the bluffs, huffing and snorting as they ran. As the last of the animals ran by, the two side ran out to meet one another. Grev's soldiers ran with spears held out, while the orcs sprinted at them with great ferocity.

Spears met the forerunners, stabbing out before the orcs could reach. But after the first wave, Grev's men stood no chance. The orcs kept their running pace as they plowed through their enemy. They hacked with their swords, mowing them down. No man was left alive by the time Gabel reached the fight. Their tents were cut down and trampled, the entire camp leveled to the dirt.

The orcs took no pause at their victory, only kept their momentum, and made pace down the road. As they marched into the Royal Plains, they came across more civilization. Field workers and shepherds stopped to stare at the battalion of warriors that walked down the way. They marveled at the long white banners that flew in the wind and the knights that carried them.

As they descended south, the weather followed them. They set up camp in the evenings and set out in the mornings. The ground grew cold and the north wind brought snow down into the land. It was light out, but the season grew ever colder into the winter. The army of the King moved east around the mountain castle and settled in the edge of the Avarwood. The officers claimed it would serve as better protection and provide the army with the resources they needed. Orcs and men stalked the forest and set up an encampment where they would garrison and plan for the assault. The ash-skinned warriors were quick to make base. Trees were cut down and forges and buildings were put into place. They fortified themselves behind the snowy hills where the eye cannot reach from the castle. After a few days passed by, they sent scouts in the dark of the night to Saint George to bring word of the King's arrival.

Around dawn, the riders entered the town, startled to find no soldiers. The hollowed-out town seemed not up to the glory it had been held. An old beggar called out to the two orcs who stood high on their horses. "What brings you so far?" The woman asked them. Puzzled, the orcs did not answer. "Why did you come so far from your homeland, surely you must be lost?"

"We travel where we please," Covering the fact they were with an army, for security's sake. "Though perhaps we are lost, is this the town of Saint George?" The beggar woman nodded. "Then where is this army we hear of?"

"They have left, taken to the olden fort of Redmont, just east of this place," The woman coughed. "The men, they raved that they would take the town as they left. If you are to find them, they will be held up there."

"Thank you, madam," The scouts turned their steeds and rode back to Fort Redmont. There the riders found them; the bodies of their enemy scattered around. The blood stained the earth. The two riders entered the city, only to be met with the pointed end of spears and swords.

"Woah there! We are riders of the King's army," The orc informed them.

"No body of Grev's has a place here!"

"Nah, we are bodies of the true King. Your King. He has sent us to seek the condition of his awaiting army."

"Forgive us, sires," Sven approached them from behind the crowd. "We're used to being the only loyalists left. Our men will be fit for another battle."

"I understand," The orc said. "And what is the state of our King's knights?"

"I, Ragnar, am here," Ragnar started. "But Sir Adir, my brother, has perished."

"Our condolences to you, sir," The orc said. Ragnar nodded. "The King himself is requesting to see his knights and whomever is in charge of this company."

"That is, I," Sven began, "lord Sven of Saint George, and his Prince Ivan," Ivan came forward, standing behind Ragnar and Sven. Alessia looked on from behind the crowd.

"We shall go to him at once," Sven announced. The men disbanded and went to gather whatever they needed for the ride. Myles shook Ivan's hand when the men dispersed.

"Good luck to you," Myles said. Ivan just smiled faintly and nodded.

Alessia came to Ragnar as he saddled his horse.

"Let me go with you," She pressed. He shook his head. "Am I to stay here in anxiety, unknowing if you'll return? You said it yourself you're stronger with me. Ragnar, what if…"

"Alessia. I'm sorry," He sighed as he embraced her and kissed her forehead, "I shall return to you. Okay?" He parted and met with the others who were being guided by the orcs to where their King was.

They rode south around Castle Rock and into the Avarwood. This region was now covered in a carpet of snow and the woods seemed void of life. They entered the camp around evening, which after this time, was named Fox Fire. Wooden palisades were put into place around the encampment and guards stood ever at the ready in case of any danger. The orcs rode past the gates, which were immediately closed and barred behind them. The men were led to a longhouse in the center of camp. It was the gathering place for officers and soldiers while waiting battle. Heavy wooden doors were opened for the knights and stood before them, their King. He set his goblet down.

"My dearest knight, how I have longed to see your face again!" He rushed to meet Ragnar and greeted him. Igran and Delwyn also stood by and welcomed their friend. They embraced and cheered to see their kin.

"You are lord Sven, am I correct?"

"Yes, my liege," Sven bowed before the King.

"Ah, I have heard of your army. I am very impressed that you took the initiative to gather men in the name of your kingdom."

"It was in your name, my King."

"Do not let your kingdom be defined by who sits at the throne. But I am flattered to be of inspiration," Sven listened. The lord then went to greet Igran and Delwyn.

Gabel looked up and saw his son, wearing his usual black doublet, standing in the door.

"Bless my soul..." Before Ivan could say anything, his father went and hugged him. "My son, have I longed most to see you," Ivan was relieved with this welcome and greeted his father the same.

That night, the men and orcs were all acquainted. The knights and officers dined in the hall, lifting their glasses to the air. Feasting on fine meats and baked foods, they all took turns telling tales of their travels.

"The troll was clearing the forest with each swing of his axe," Delwyn had everyone emersed. "It would have eaten our horse whole if the four of us didn't bring the beast down. I believe it was Igran who cut his heart just to get his fair share of action."

"Is that true?" Gabel turned to Igran.

"Every word," The knight shrugged. The room filled with laughter.

"A troll is nothing! You should have seen the size of the man they brought out against us at Redmont. The mammoth was at least seven feet tall, built like a bear," Sven waved his arms. Those at the table roared. "He held two flails in one hand! This man was a *beast*."

"Was this the lord that killed Adir?" Igran asked Ragnar. The room feel quiet.

"Aye. Bramus, lord of Frostford. He was every bit as perilous as Sven says. But the world learned something that day…" Ragnar looked intently at the men. "There is nothing under the sun that two Stoneram brothers could not vanquish!" He beat his chest with a smirk. They all roared again. "I pummeled that bastard into the ground and left a crater the size of his realm right into his skull!" The knights and orcs raised glasses and bantered with one another.

"My son," King Gabel eventually turned to his right, "You are terribly quiet. What of you? What has happened since we've been apart?"

Ivan took a deep breath. He looked up at Sven, who nodded for him to go on.

"But where to start? Grev imprisoned me and my sister. Evangeline had stood up to him in all his wickedness. Father, she has your guts. She was not afraid to face death, and surely, I thought she must have died for her courage. He took her away when she stood up to him. He killed Sir Ulfer, too. That I know for sure. Grev holds such wicked powers and he used them to torture anyone who did not bow at his will. Eventually, I challenged Grev and had nearly lost my own life. He had this blade of fire, a cursed weapon. I beat him enough to make my escape. I stole a horse and rode all the way to Saint George. News of their army put fear in Grev and his men," He smiled lightly. All around the table, looks of empathy went out to Ivan for all he had gone through.

"Son do not keep me in anxiety. Is your sister alive?"

"I believed until late that she had been executed. Grev convinced me he had done it with his own hand. But I was told that she is still alive. I shouldn't have left her there. I didn't know she was still in that horrible place until after I escaped."

"Ivan, my son, we will get your sister back. Don't blame yourself, for I do not blame you for any of this. Only he is to be blamed. You must hear me, don't beat yourself up. If you are *that* angry, learn to channel it. Use that rage on the battlefield, not in your head. Let Grev know that you will strike him down for what he has done. Let that devil know that throughout this storm of misery, you are more unyielding. My son, I am proud of what you have lived through, you will make a fine heir to the throne."

Ivan released some tears in joy. Hearing the words of his father. The rest of the company around the table raised their goblets and cheered. "For the King and for the Realm!"

"Now get rest. In the morning, there is war," Orubark stood and announced. The others agreed and started to clear out from the hall.

"Ragnar," Gabel said. "Take Lord Sven back to his men. Let them know tomorrow we'll be storming the castle."

"Yes sir," Ragnar stood to leave, Sven followed behind.

"There's an army out there," Barris said from where he stood along the city wall. Light from within the camp glowed in the snowy night. "I'd say we take them now. Hit em by surprise."

"You heard the orders," Bosa also kept his gaze on their enemy's camp. "Stay here and stay warm. Let them freeze outside the castle walls."

"We're freezing now. At least they got a fire. You should go find a mage. Have em keep us warm."

"Relax. Soon enough heat will be their enemy."

The Siege, part 1

The following day, the knights rallied and formed ranks. Snow fell in heavy flakes and froze to the soldier's armor. Their metal boots packed down the snow as they prepared themselves in their camp. The orcs hit their fists together and braced themselves in the cold morning. Behind the army, tall constructs were being rolled out of the wood.

"Will they work?" Gabel asked the War Chief.

"Do you doubt my craftsmen? The trebuchets will open the gates if the cowards inside won't," Orubark said.

"You best be right."

Lines of orcs marched out of the grey forest. They raised their banners and shields of white and silver. Snow from the ground packed itself in between their plates of armor and melted against their skin. Years of leading battle in the cold months of winter hardened the orc fights. They did not even shiver at the falling snow. The King, the Prince, Sir Igran, Sir Delwyn, and Sir Orubark rode their steeds in front of the foot soldiers as they marched toward the castle.

Atop the watchtowers and walls of the city, guards scanned the earth below. Flurries of snow took away their visibility, they only saw the harsh atmosphere they were in. Coming into their view was a man dressed in black armor. The guards rang the bells in their towers as they kept view of their lone enemy.

"It's the prince!" Grev's men called out. "Archers at your posts!" Men in violet moved through the cold, white streets of their city. Vapor blew from their mouths as they hustled in their armor. They placed themselves between ramparts and in windows. Nocking their arrows, they readied their bows for the man to step in range. Then behind Ivan, from the blizzard, an army appeared. Hundreds of soldiers in shimmering white armor marched out of the clouds and flurries as if the divine had placed them there.

"Prepare for an attack! Prepare yourselves!" As bells rang throughout the empty city, soldiers were gathering by the gates and forming in the streets.

"Over here!" On the opposing side of the city another army, dressed in mismatched leather and iron, came from the cold haze. The hundreds of men from Saint George formed ranks before the city gates. They huddled close to one another and griped their steel weapons as they crossed over the frozen farmland.

"Look, in the distance!" Back where the King's army stood, wooden contraptions were rolled out of the snowy cloud. They were tall, each had an arm that was pulled back against a counterweight. From the end of the long arm was a sling which held a massive stone. More complex than a catapult, the guards quickly observed.

"Be ready for fire!" An order rang out over the soldiers.

Down in the snowfields, the King consulted with his knights from atop his horse.

"We take the attack in stages, I warn you though, my castle was built to withstand a siege."

"A bit late to be prideful, father?" Ivan chuckled.

"Don't you worry," Orubark turned to Gabel, "there is nothing that can be created that cannot destroyed!" They waved for his men to bring the machines into action. "May it bring forth the wrath of this kingdom!"

The munitioners released the mechanism on the trebuchet. Which brought the weight falling downward, causing the arm and the sling to be thrown skyward. The sling released its heavy boulder, hurdling toward the castle. It hit the outer wall, cratering the face. Bricks shook out of place and fell to the earth.

"Hold!" Soldiers were ordered along the ramparts. Orubark signaled for the other to be launched. It flew overhead, dealing more damage to the fortifications. The men worked in the snow to load another shot. Using heavy beams to roll the boulders out of the forest.

"Advance!" Gable ordered and kicked his horse to start walking. A banner was raised for the command and the orcs marched steadily toward the city. More boulders were hurled at the great wall, over the heads of the approaching soldiers. The moat around the castle was frozen over, rendering it useless to the defenders. The falling rubble broke through the frozen river but filled the water quickly with debris.

The foot soldiers got into thin lines and waited for the final blasts. For once the wall was broken, the King's army would be running in through the gap. With each strike of the stone, more creases formed on the ancient wall, sending archers falling off the side. The army below were close enough now that archers could fire down at them.

The orcs uniformly made a blockade by joining their shields over their heads. As the final stone fell and as the rubble settled, the sounds of horns could be heard. War horns were being played as a que for the division to charge. They dropped their shields and made good pace for the opening. Arrows still hailed down on them, striking exposed necks and limbs. Yet the majority of the swordsmen got through. After the first wave, the King and his knights rode through on their horses. Another division was already coming behind them. They ran through the snow-dusted ground toward where their enemies had gathered. The orcs flooded into the narrow sectors between the outer walls. Barricades were set up by Grev's men. Their long spears jabbed out at the orcs before they're swords could reach them. They stood behind wooden barricades, but the enormous number of soldiers eventually broke through.

Saint George's army at this time was also moving forward. Snow collected on their brows and frost formed in their beards. Their eyes were set on taking the main gate. The men held their shields high as they marched up the road. They began to pick up pace as they neared the city walls, raising their shields as arrows started to rain down on them. The army carried with them a battering ram, which was covered by iron plates at the top to protect the handlers from archers. Arrows plinked off the iron as the men ran ahead of their army. Ten men of great strength threw the ram up against the closed doors. The weapon only dented the gate's wooden construction. Arrows were now being fired in at them from further down the high wall. When one of the carriers was shot down, he was quickly replaced by another soldier. They ran again to strike the barricade. Cracks were sent up the great gates and splinters shot out on either side.

Fighters from atop the gate rolled out a cauldron, the soldiers below only noticed when black pitch was already poured down on them. The boiling liquid consumed the attackers. It burned into their muscle to where they could no longer stand. They dropped the ram and fell back. A few wizards from atop the wall threw fire down onto the black tar, igniting it in flame. Archers took full advantage of this opportunity, pelting down on the men. The burning tar melted the snow as it burned down the road. Archers from the ground fired back at those on the castle wall.

"Break the gates!" Sven yelled from his horse.

Hardy men pushed forward again. They rushed toward the gate again, over the flames and picked up the ram that their brothers had dropped. The grips still scorching, and the front had caught fire. Men hoisted the battering ram off the ground and charged at the gate. They broke through and barreled into the streets. The army was met with lines of defending soldiers, who charged to meet them. The men with the battering ram kept the charge, breaking through a sharpened barricade.

Alessia was in the forefront, breaking past the line of spearheads and chopping at their enemies from close range. Alessia turned to dodge a spear jutting towards her. As she twisted back, she brought her blade with her, striking her attacker. She turned her sword and struck the man again. The army pushed under the next gate, but the portcullis dropped shut on them. Some of the front line were now cut off from the rest of their army. Soldiers were now pinned against the heavy iron bars.

"Up the stairs, to the lever!" One man shouted. Alessia took up the call and followed up to the ramparts. Archers that were firing down on the fight turned to the attackers running up the stairs. Alessia and the other swordsmen didn't halt their charge but swung to strike them down, breaking their bows. They pushed to the top of the gate and found the crank that lifted the metal portcullis. Alessia heaved and brought the final defense out of the way.

Men ran deeper into the streets of their capital and worked uphill to engage their foes; whose forces were waiting for them. Their numbers filled the street as the marched down at the attackers. They held out their halberds and spears to stab those who ran up at them, yet some men of Saint George broke through the defenders and started attacking at close range. Even now that the men were close enough to fight, they still had an uphill fight. Sven and Ragnar came through on their horses yet stopped at the sight of the spearmen.

"I know a way around them," Ragnar called. They steered into the alley and went around the main road, where all the fighting was. They appeared behind Grev's forces, none of which noticing the threat behind them. Ragnar and Sven took advantage of their blindness and drove their horses and weapons to the backs of these men. Ragnar swung his warhammer and knocked a man unconscious from behind. The soldiers turned in surprise to meet their new foes. The forces of Saint George pressed the gap and soon defeated the division that fought between them.

In one household up the street, an elderly man turned over his furnishings. He looked under his bed and between the rafters.

"Why do you do this? Husband answer me!" His wife asked pleaded him. From behind a cupboard, the old man pulled out an iron sword which he had hidden.

"Those men out there, they are fighting for our good. For us!" He said excitedly. "I would be ashamed if I didn't raise my sword in defense of my kingdom!" With that, he charged out of his humble house into the chaos of the streets. He blindsided a soldier in violet and thrusted his sword into him.

Both the King's army and the army of Saint George were in full force now. The men and orcs pushed uphill to the inner circle. Most of Grev's forces stood in the large market squares, waiting for the fight to reach them. The armies charged to meet each other. Men and orcs fought with and against one another. They shivered below their cold steel armor, battling to gain footholds of the city.

"Myles!" Ivan called out to the smith as he saw him across the street, battling with the sword that shown like silver, Dawnsmist.

"Yes, your highness?" He shouted back, not taking his concentration off his opponents.

"You told me my sister is alive."

"Aye," Myles yelled.

"Then how about we rescue her?" Myles nodded and followed as they left the fight. They went through alleys and climbed the sides of buildings to sneak into the inner circle. As they pulled themselves over the ramparts and onto the wall, they were found in between several archers. One shot from close range, but Myles swatted the bow out of the way as he charged. Ivan fought the other way, slashing down the guards who had no close quarter weaponry to defend themselves.

"Come on!" Ivan started to run along the wall. They bashed and pushed archers off the sides as they made their way further into the city. They slashed all the way to the garden walls outside the palace. Ivan sheathed his sword and grabbed onto the thick vines that grew up the white stone. Myles kept watch behind them before sheathing the King's Sword and climbing up himself. Dropping down to the courtyard, they noticed they were alone. Only sounds of battle faded into the garden. In the brief moment they had, they realized how heavy the snow was falling that day. They rushed up to the heavy double doors of the castle, which creaked as they slowly opened. Even the great hall lay empty.

Their armor echoed off the high arched ceiling as they ran down the hall. Sunlight peered through widows and illuminated the dust in the air around empty throne. But the two did not stop to look. They made quick to the cellar door, Myles grabbing the set of keys hanging just outside. Ivan threw open the door and looked down the dark set of stairs. The dungeon was dim and frosted over. The two teens could once again see their breaths.

"Evangeline?" Ivan called before taking in the room.

"Ivan!" A voice erupted from the corner. The princess leapt to her feet and grabbed the iron bars between them.

"We're getting you out of here, m'lady," Myles unlocked the door. Evangeline hugged and kissed him on the cheek as she left the cell, then went to hug her brother.

"I thought you'd been killed," She held him tight.

"Grev convinced me of the same. If not for Myles, I would not have known you were alive," Ivan stepped back and held her shoulders. "Now come on, we need to go."

"Okay," She nodded.

The three ran up to the great hall. Across the room, in front of them, stood what looked like a phantom. It glowed softly as it stood alone, still as a statue. It wore a dark cloak that seem to radiate a black magic. The mage then turned to them. He had eyes that glowed like fire and skin that was charred and tight to the bone. The mage pulled his fiery sword into existence as he stared them down.

"Get her out of here," Ivan drew his blade.

"I'm not leaving you," Myles unsheathed his own.

"Do as I say. Get Evangeline to safety," Ivan began walking toward the old evil foe. Myles grabbed the princess by the arm and ran behind the pillars toward the front doors.

"Does the boy prince challenge me again?" Grev pointed the sword of flames at him.

"Damn right, you old hag. Come on!" Ivan shouted. Grev charged at him, his sword leaving a trail of embers. Their blades clashed and shot out through the castle.

Myles ran down the steps of the courtyard, keeping the King's Sword held up to defend the princess as they fled. He cracked open the garden gate and saw only a handful of soldiers fighting on the other side.

"Are you ready, princess?" He turned and asked. His copper hair hanging down in his face. He pushed open the gate and stood in front of her as they kept along the wall. Several men noticed and ran at them. Myles stepped forward and redirected their blades, countering and striking one down. The other lunged at Evangeline, but his blade was forced into the earth by Myles' sword. The smith cut up and slayed him. Looking around, the two continued into the alley ways and moved down the mountain.

King Gabel and his men were pushing up the streets. He swung the bronze greatsword to strike down his enemies. They fell to the icy road beneath them. But for every soldier the King and his men had slayed, more would rush to fill their place. Fighting uphill in the heavy snow, even the elements were against him.

"Fire!" Harlow ordered and pointed through the clouded streets. Through the haze the fight could only be heard.

"Sir, our own men are down there," One soldier along the wall protested.

"Are you deaf? Fire down on them! We cannot let Gabel reach the palace."

"Yes sir."

Out of the flurries of snow, raging fire was hurled. Gabel ducked but the fireball sent some of his men to the ground. More fire fell down on them, burning up the freezing air as they passed. Knights fighting through frostbite were now engulfed in flames. Even Grev's soldiers were caught in the fire. Arrows now fell onto them, too.

"Hold yourselves!" Gabel ordered. In the chaos of fighters, there was no clear line. Only a mass of fighting men and orcs. From the walls and the cliffside of the castle, mages shot down on them. Ragnar raised his shield to block incoming fire. He stood steadfast, but the force of the impact pushed him back over the cobble streets. He lowered his shield and at once swung his hammer to knock a man's hips out from under him. He then swung down and pounded in the man's breastplate. Seeing two soldiers cutting at Igran, Ragnar raised his shield and plowed forward, knocking them over. The two knights then kicked and chopped at their downed enemies.

Orubark duel-wielded axes, striking with intense rhythm. If a man could block one of his blades, he couldn't block the next. The orc grunted and yelled with each attack, flashing his sharp canine teeth. His orcs with his did not flinch or shiver at the cold as their opponents did. Yet even these expert warriors could not withstand the wrath of fire that rained down on them.

Delwyn lifted his shield to defend himself. Spears and swords cut at the deep gash in the shield. With each impact, Delwyn heard a crack split through the wood and steel. He retaliated by slashing at them, trying to push their swords away from both himself and his shield. Finally, one spear was jut out from the mass of fighters and split the shield in half. Delwyn staggered back as the two pieces fell off his arm. He was left now with just his sword. Though he was exhausted from the long battle, his hand froze to his sword. Freed from the weight of his shield, Delwyn felt a second wind and began fighting with more speed.

The blusters of snow were burned out of the air as a man consumed in fire appeared on the streets. The atmosphere seem to pause in that moment. Fire and magic swirled around this man in a dark cloak. Wings of fire flew from his back. He left a trail of embers as he walked down the road. All the armies stood frozen at the sight as this man ignited a sword of flames.

"By gods," One of the soldiers said in horror, "It's Grev!"

"Grev is dead!" The mage called. "I, the Infernal King, am beyond death. Bow to me now, for there is no being who can stop me. Bow to me, army of Gabel and I shall accept your surrender!"

Even Grev's army shook and cowered. They held their blades out at Gabel's army, looking for them to obey. The knights and their King stood tall. Some of their soldiers looked to each other for what to do.

"We will never bend our knees to a monster!" One of the orcs called out.

"Then taste hell!" From Grev's hand, he formed a ball of fire greater than any of the other mages. He cast it toward them. It exploded in a blaze, setting fire even to the ground. He threw another and another. His blasts shook the buildings nearby and caused them to crack and fall. Fire shot up the stone walls more devastating than dragon's breath. The attackers scrambled to their feet and ran to get away. Grev's men charged them down. Their spears went through the men and orcs who were already burning up.

"Sir we need to get out of here!" Igran called to Gabel, who nodded firmly. "Fall back! Everyone, fall back!" The King's army ran down the hill, where more guards garrisoned and waited for them. The knights found their horses, pushed down the streets and fought through their attackers. Grev raised his palms and then brought them downward. With their fall, he brought buildings down on the men who tried to flee. Grev's army closed in and slaughtered those trapped in the rubble. The knights, led by Gabel, escaped through the hole they blew into the castle walls. They retreated back to their camp in the forest. Other survivors managed to stagger out, finding whatever exit they could. All made their way to Fox Fire.

"Dammit!" The King yelled as he jumped off his horse. "Damn it all!" He knocked over a weapons rack in fury. He stormed into his tent and for a brief moment all was silent. Then the survivors found their way back. The medical tents filled, most came with lacerations and burns, others suffered more mortal wounds. Healers were quick to start working. Gold glowing magic left their hands as they worked to save the wounded.

Other survivors were simply sitting outside on the ground. Igran was going through the camp, trying to get a sense of their defeat.

"Sven how many men have you?" Igran asked. The lord shook his head as he moved past.

"Ivan? Has anyone seen the prince? Has anyone seen Ivan?" Most people were looking for their own comrades or in too much pain to give mind to the knight.

"There is no sign of him," Orubark coughed.

Sir Delwyn staggered into the camp. He ripped his helmet off and gasped in shock. The young knight didn't even notice the severe burn on his arm.

"Is this it?" He asked, looking around to see maybe a few dozen soldiers left. Soon Ragnar rode in. On the back of his horse was a woman soldier who was crying out in pain.

"Don't worry, you're going to be ok, lass," He spoke to Alessia as he carried her. "Stay with me, ok?"

"Yes, sir," She nodded and yelled out to relieve some anguish. The healers rushed to her and removed her armor to find that she had been stuck in the side with an arrow. Ragnar left the healers to do their work, looking back several times as he left the tent. Between the wooden gates a young man came in, a lady in a dress wrapped around his arm. Gabel stopped when he saw a familiar scarlet dress.

"Evangeline," Gabel rushed to her and brought her close in a hug. "My daughter."

She teared up but found no words to say.

"Is this your rescuer then?" He put his hand on Myles's shoulder.

"With Ivan, too. He took on Grev so we could get away."

"Damn boy has my guts," Gabel rubbed his face, trying to keep in his mixture of emotions. "Is that my sword?" He pointed to the sheath around Myles's hip.

"Yes, sir," He unclipped the belt and held it out. "It presented itself to me when I needed it most. Ivan dueled me for it, but I dare not resist the King."

"No, son. It's yours," Gabel pushed the sword back toward Myles.

"We lost almost everyone in that final blow, there is no way we could regain that ground," Orubark started that night. The knights and officers were gathered in the longhouse. "How many soldiers do we have left?"

"How do we even fight against that kind of power?" Sven added. "The orc's right, we wouldn't even get close. Grev brought hell upon the earth."

"How many of his men did he lose? They can't have much more defensemen left, can they?" Ragnar shook. The men all looked to the king who stood apart from them. Torchlight shone softly off his crown.

"I know that at this point, it is near impossible," Gabel sighed, "but you cannot give up on me now."

"Give up on you? No. Never. But seriously doubt our survival? Maybe," Delwyn said honestly. "Look, we'll fight with you, whatever we decide to do next, but what can even be done at this point?"

"Cut off their resources," Igran weighed in. "We may not have enough men for another assault, but we can stop them from getting food."

"I still have people in that city," Gabel shook his head. "I won't starve them out with the enemy."

"Maybe we should wait for another attack. Rebuild our numbers," Sven said.

"And then have Grev blast them into oblivion just like he did to us?" Ragnar refuted. "No. We need to do something different."

A soldier ran into the longhouse.

"Forgive me, sires, but they've sent someone here to speak with you."

Gabel exchanged looked with his knights then went to see. He grabbed his old sword from Myles and tied its sheath around his waist. They followed the soldier to the camp's wall and looked out to see one of Grev's officers who had been escorted by guards in purple cloaks. Gabel walked out from the gate. His knights remained close behind, keeping their hands on the hilt of their swords. The guards dismounted their horses and walked out to meet Gabel.

"Grev has sent me to discuss terms for you and your men," Officer Harlow bowed his head slightly.

"I am surprised he would be so diplomatic," Gabel replied.

"Our king can be reasonable man. Now, may we go into the woods to talk," Harlow suggested, looking at the archers along the walls who took aim at him. "For more neutral ground."

"Very well," The King turned and walked along side Harlow. They went aways into the forest, away from the eyes of the camp. The ground was white, packed with snow and the trees were bare and frosted.

"Might I ask, who has Grev sent to me?"

"My name is Harlow. One of Grev's chief officers," The man with the scarred face answered. His guards were lagging behind the two as they strolled through the woods.

"Were in the rebellion?" Gabel asked.

"I was, some thirty years ago. My brothers all died in Three Mile March. You defeated Grev that day, did you know? He commanded the whole rebellion. Then he patiently waited and endured until the time was right."

Gabel didn't respond, only walking along further.

"And now, Grev has sent me to negotiate terms of surrender. The tides have shifted. You see, he has prisoners that he is willing to release if you turn yourself in," Harlow continued.

"And my knights?"

"He's only interested in you," He replied.

"And if I do not turn myself in?" Gabel asked.

"He will kill all of the prisoners. Should I mention your son is among them? But it's up to you."

The King drew his sword and held the tip of the blade to Harlow's neck. Its silver edge glowed like the moon. Harlow's guards scrabbled for their weapons but were surrounded by the King's elite knights who came out from the trees with their swords drawn. Harlow held his chin up, seeing there was nothing he could do.

"Get on your knees," Gabel said to the officer. He obeyed and slowly dropped to the snow. "I've heard what you have to say. Hear now my terms. First, you should know that there is no 'neutral ground.' I am High King of the Realms and this will always be my land. You all are going to die here, and your blood will stain the snow. Then I am going to walk in the front gate and kill Grev and take back *my* kingdom. Does anyone have an issue with that?" Gabel's knights shook their heads as they held their swords at the throats of the guards. "Do you accept my terms?" He asked.

"That is preposterous. You can't expect to win, Grev is too strong."

The King swung his weapon and slashed Harlow's neck. His blood sprinkled the white ground.

The Siege, part 2

The next morning was dead. A fresh layer of frost covered the bodies that lay on the ruined grounds of Castle Rock. Crows picked at the corpses, hoping along the ground. No one moved about. No guard spoke, haven been through such a bloody attack. Most had not slept that night. There was hardly any one left to give orders, they didn't know whether or not to stand their post. Most of Grev's men were simply trying to find a place to get out of the snow, huddling in the watchtowers or in abandoned buildings in the market. Up in the courtyard before the castle, a ring of guards were standing around the mage and his prisoner.

"I should be expecting his arrival shortly," Grev turned to Prince Ivan, who was chained to the ground and stripped of his armor. "And when he comes, I shall make an example of him." The Prince lifted his head and glared at his foe. "And then, I will kill everyone he has ever known."

"I don't think you know who you're really up against. They will come for you, I assure you, they will come. You can kill my father, but his men will come next. You may kill him, but *his* kingdom will never die. His knights and his men will come for you, relentlessly and unyielding. They will strike again and again. They will siege this castle day after day, like rain that will drown out every flame you've ever made!" Grev backed up and left him without a word. "A hard rain is coming for you, Grev. You have never been less ready."

Across the forest, the King mounted his horse. Guards cuffed Gabel in chains, who wore his crown high on his head. The guards wore their purple cloaks with hoods covering their faces from the bitter wind. They were mounted on steeds as well, which all had chains connecting to the King's horse. Each breath could be seen in the cold air. All of Gabel's soldiers gathered in the camp to see him be taken. No one spoke as they watched their King led away in chains.

"For the King!" One shouted. The guards stopped and turned to see who it was.

"For the King!" Another hollered.

"For the King!" More joined in.

"For the King! For the King!" They bellowed. Gabel took in the sight, then looked forward to the castle.

"For the King! For the King! For the King!"

The guards kicked their horses and left. The camp ever chanting behind them. The horses trotted through the deep snow, kicking up bluffs as they rode. The battered gate was opened as they neared.

"Let Grev know he is here," A watchmen turned to another. The guards in violet cloaks kept close to their prisoner. Once inside the quiet city, the horses walked slowly. Peasants and soldiers shuffled out to see the King be paraded up his own castle. They went under old banners that once flew high and now hung torn. The cavalcade went up the streets and walked ever slowly past the remaining townsfolk of the city. No one spoke, the townsfolk only mourned. Eventually, they approached the high gate of the inner circle which surrounded the palace.

"Adonai help me," Gabel muttered as the gate was opened. Grev was standing on the other side, in the middle of the courtyard.

"The usurped King returns to his castle a prisoner," Grev held a blade to Ivan's neck. "Now who is lord of all?"

"Here I am," King Gabel called out, lifting his shackles. "Now let him go."

"I had almost forgotten about our accord," Grev spoke. "But I got to thinking. The last time I intended to execute one of your children, a knight got in the way. I regret letting his pitiful death be in place for hers. I won't deprive myself the satisfaction now!" Grev tugged up on Ivan's black curls and pressed the blade closer to his neck.

"No!" Gabel pleaded. The prince took a deep breath which could be heard over the silent tension. He looked up at his father with the fire of rage in his eyes.

"You give him hell," Ivan yelled. The blade on Ivan's throat glided across his flesh and split it open. The prince fell instantly.

"Ivan!" King Gabel cried at the scene. Just then the mounted guards, who escorted Gabel, removed their over cloaks. The purple cloaks blowing away in the wind. It was the King's knights, Delwyn, Ragnar, Igran, Sven, and Orubark, all in sterling armor. They drew their swords and kicked at their steeds to charge. The King broke free of his brittle, fake chains and drew his greatsword as well, which has been concealed.

The knights and their King gave out a war cry that echoed through the ancient city. A cry that woke the crows and shook the men in their tracks. The six charged, hooves sparked against the stone. Grev's men from all around bolted at the knights on horseback. As the horsemen drove forward, they mowed their enemies down. Swinging their swords and stopping every guard that came near.

Grev gripped his sword, now catching flame, along with his eyes. It burned with wrath and hatred. It melted the winter ground as he walked towards Gabel. The King dismounted his horse and holding his greatsword in his hands, approached his long rival. The two glared each other down as they neared. Grev the Infernal swung down at the King. As his blade struck Gabel's, a fiery burst of magic energy shot out. Sparks fell but did not phase King Gabel; he stood firm in his place. The King returned a blow. The two went back and forth violently, each strike sending out sparks.

The knights were on foot at this point and clashed with the guards. Sir Delwyn still wielded the sword from Thundertree, which still had the blue cloth tied on the end. He fought with passion for his kingdom and for everything he cared of. In the short months he'd been away, he had grown quite so. He was an experienced fighter now, like Igran and his fellow knights. To them, he was no longer an outsider or a newcomer. He was in the ranks with them. He fought at their backs and they fought at his. Delwyn continued to struggle against the oncoming guards, striking them with the edge of his blade.

Close by was Orubark who collided with his foes. No amount of training could outmatch the orc's full-born raw power; for a blow from his axes would stagger any man. From the corner of his eye, he could see that Igran had fallen. A purple soldier raised his spear to burrow into the knight's chest. In a splinter of time, Orubark pivoted on his foot and swung upward to deflect the opposing weapon. As he continued the revolution of his axe, Orubark lashed across this man's face. With one arm, he picked his comrade from the ground, with the other, continued to swipe at his foes.

Ragnar and Sven found themselves with their backs against the city wall as they were outnumbered more than the rest of the knights. They picked up fallen shields and glanced off incoming attacks. Ragnar looked over at Sven, who was never so hard pressed in a battle before. His inexperience caused him to be shaky and flinch more.

"I'll push them off, you cover me!" Ragnar ordered. Sven looked up at him with doubt, but then nodded in compliance. Ragnar braced his shield and pushed off the wall behind him. He plowed through the lines of soldiers. Sven struck down those who tried to come from the sides, but he couldn't stop them all.

A spearhead slipped through the plates of Sven's armor and cut deep into his side. The shock of pain went up his spine and deep into his bones. His sword slipped from his fingers. In his charge, he stumbled to his knees. His sweat soaked hair dangled down to his face. As he braced himself to get up, he was met by the blade of another spear. They stabbed repeatedly, and Sven screamed with his last breaths. Ragnar was close and threw down the guardsmen. He put his hammer through neck of the nearest soldier. He struck the remaining guards in vengeance, not allowing any of them to stand again.

Gabel was still in combat with Grev. They slashed at each other skillfully. Though Gabel could block much with the great bronze sword, he could not swing it as fast as his enemy. Grev swiped at his legs, then quickly brought his sword overhead. Gabel wasn't able to get his sword up in time to stop Grev from striking down on his him. The fiery sword rang as it ricocheted backward, blocked not by Gabel's sword, but with his crown. The gold and silver crown broke in half and fell to the ground. Gabel remained unharmed from the attack.

"I have shattered your crown," Grev smirked.

"But you will not break this kingdom," Gabel glared down his foe. "For you fight with sword and flame, but you will be beaten down by the Almighty."

"Never!" Grev yelled and breathed fire upon the King. He was soon surrounded in flame. Gabel staggered backwards, his clothes still burning. Grev breathed out fire into the air, wings of flame grew at his back and his eyes ignited once more. His hands were ever burning, the fire charring even his robes. Grev shot this fire at the King, blasting him relentlessly. The heat scorched the King's cape and burned at his skin. Gabel let out grunts of pain as he tried to hold up his weapon.

"You're weak!" Grev began to taunt. He slashed his sword down and was barely blocked by Gabel's. Delwyn saw this and pushed his way through the soldiers, closer to the scene. "And you are going to die here."

"My King!" Delwyn cried as he saw Gabel burning up.

Grev attacked in flurries now, seeing the King was weakened. With burning muscle, Gable lost all strength to wield his greatsword. As Grev struck again, Gabel dropped his weapon. The bronze sword clanging as it hit the stone. Grev brought his sword across Gabel's stomach, leaving a burning gash. Grev dispelled his sword as the King fell to his knees. Grev turned back to the palace. As he did so, he was caught off guard by the burning gaze of Sir Delwyn who was in mid-swing. And with one mighty cleave of his sword, he took off Grev's head.

As the mage's body fell lifelessly to the ground, all the curses in his body drifted away, the soul of the dragon now gone. As the last of his soldiers had fallen to the knight's hands, the scene became quiet. Sir Delwyn still stood over the body of his enemy. He glared down at him as his hair covered his eyes now. He looked up to see the knights standing around their fallen King, looking back at him. Ragnar had recovered Ivan's body where it had been trampled in the battle.

"It's done, lad," Igran spoke softly to him. "It's done." Delwyn let his sword fall from his hands, which had still been clenched. He relaxed his body, taking deep breathes of relief.

"We couldn't save him," Delwyn began to choke up.

"No," Orubark shook his head. "We did not."

"So, this kingdom has no King now," Ragnar said. "No King and no heir," He looked over to Sven's body. "Even the best ruler among the lords is gone."

The Successor

Remnants of the King's men were called into the city. They came in with their swords, but no guard challenged them. They wanted no fight. Once news reached the guards that Grev was dead, they left their stations. Villagers started cleaning off the ruined roads and buildings. The shuffling of feet was among the only sounds heard. Soldiers helped clear rubble off of the streets and removing dead bodies from the city. Barris walked down the road that spiraled around the mountain. He moved slow as he looked over the corpses on the ground. Going up the stairs and onto the wall, he crossed an archway that led to one of the watchtowers. He went down the tower stairs and back into the street. He recognized a lot of the men in purple but could not find his brother. After giving up his search, Barris took the purple sash off his armor and let it drop to the snow. He looked up to see two people coming up the road. Barris looked over his shoulder to see if anyone else was watching him, then he disappeared into the alley.

Myles turned to see where the soldier went, but he was gone. He warmed Evangeline's hand as they continued up the streets with the other survivors. The two made their way up to the garden. Igran saw them and turned to wave for the princess to stop. But it was too late, she had already seen her father and brother's bodies lying on the stone. She dropped to the ground and wept. Myles knelt down to hold her, but there was nothing he could do. She sobbed profusely, doubled over, and threw up. The knights took the bodied out of sight, preparing them to be buried. The princess clung to Myles as he continued to sit with her on the frosted ground.

Sometime later, the knights were in the palace hall, by the warmth of the fire. No other light was lit. They could see snow covering the windows and blowing in the air outside.

"They will expect us to know what should happen next," Igran said to his remaining companions.

"We need to hold a funeral for Gabel and the prince. Give the city time to grieve. From then, we can determine what is to come. How to rebuild," Ragnar pitched in.

"Rebuild?" Delwyn asked. "I'm sorry, but there's nothing left here. The city's lost. Yes, we should hold the funerals, but let's face it. There's no one left to live here."

"What are you talking about? Of course, we'll rebuild," Ragnar looked to differ to his other knights.

"Delwyn's right," Igran said. "Castle Rock is destroyed. It would take generations to bring it back. It's not something we can do."

"Are you serious?" Ragnar pleaded.

"Who's going to rule?" Igran snapped. "We've no one! Everyone's-" The knight cut himself short and put his hand over his mouth. "Maybe someday, but not now. I think it is time for us to disperse."

"What? You want to disband?" Ragnar asked.

"We cannot protect this kingdom if we all remain here," Igran said. "There are lands with no lords. Saint George, Haul, The Avarwood, Frostford. A large portion of this kingdom now lay ungoverned. I think it best we take ourselves to serve there."

"We're hardly governing rulers, Igran. We're warriors," Delwyn added.

"You are knights of the High King of the Realm. That means you already have lived with justice and discernment. As far as I'm concerned, that's what it takes."

"But we will be so far," Delwyn replied. "Without our comrades, I-"

"We are not leaving each other, lad," Igran put his hand on his shoulder. "We'll just be some distance. But we still have an oath to each other and this kingdom. Dispersed, but not disbanded."

"We stand for our kingdom where it needs us most," Ragnar nodded. "Igran's right."

That evening as the sun set over the city walls, the knights led a procession down the streets. In horse-drawn carts they pulled three coffins covered in flowers. On a horse of her own was the princess, walking in front of the line. Horns blew in crestfallen tunes as the knights walked slowly down the streets. Villagers and soldiers came out to pay their respects. On the outside of the walls, away from the gate was a great tomb where knights, noblemen, and royalty were laid to rest. Through the corridors the line proceeded, carrying the bodies of the King and his prince. A tomb for Gabel was already fashioned out of white stone, his old coat of arms was carved into the lid of the sarcophagus. Two smaller tombs were also crafted and laid at the king's left and right. They removed two of the lids, and then placed the coffins into the stone tombs. The knights all lifted the stone slabs to seal the bodies away.

"These men died for their kingdom. Even through their times of doubt and pain, they persevered. An honorable death makes up for a life of mistakes… I wish I knew what God he prayed to," Igran managed to summon some words before exiting. The other knights followed him out.

Sven was also buried among the tomb of honorable knights. His name was not yet even carved into the stone. Ragnar remained there after the other knights had left the catacombs. He tapped the lid of the sarcophagus, thinking of what to say.

"Get a drink with my brother for me."

They made their way back to the great hall. The King's remnant were all gathered to hear what conclusion had been reached. Igran stood among the knights as he began to speak from a piece of parchment paper.

"The war has left this kingdom in desperate need of leadership. The remaining knights of the King, including myself, have decided that we cannot lead from the position of the throne. We simply cannot fill the role Gabel had in the Realms, not from here. There are vacancies among the lord's halls. Four realms without a ruler. We propose, being there are four of us knights, that each of us be established as lord over a realm."

The people in attendance turned to one another in loud clamor, some throwing their hands up at the idea.

"Quiet!" Ragnar hollered. Alessia stood next to him in the crowd. "Let the man speak."

"We are not interested in taking these positions to become slothful rulers. We do not intend to gorge ourselves on self-indulgences. But continue to live out chivalry and justice as we did when we served the King. I promise you any coin we make will be put back to rebuilding this kingdom. There is no party more interested in restoring the Realms than us. So, if you will, please hear what we are proposing. Chief Orubark will extend his domain of the Orcish Realm to the city of Haul and the Lake Realm. Sir Delwyn will be lord of the Avarwood, his homeland. Sir Ragnar will be lord of the Saint George and the Highland realms. I will go to Frostford and try to regain the west. This is the best solution to this kingdom's catastrophic loss of leaders."

"What of Castle Rock? Are the plains to be forgotten?" Someone shouted.

"With no prince to be crowned King, the right to rule the plains is left to a fifth lord," Igran announced. "That honor will go to Princess Evangeline."

"Be ruled by a girl? That is outrageous. It's unheard of!" A villager shouted.

"There have been lords younger than the princess in these Realms. If you do not like it, you are free to move to The Avarwood, I'm sure Sir Delwyn could use the help," Igran shot back. The rowdy villagers huffed and calmed down.

Evangeline stepped forward.

"I do just wish to stay and help the city rebuild. Castle Rock has enough resources, if the plains need support, we would be able to provide," she said.

"The lady should not have to defend her honor before you. It goes without saying the palace is hers. She is wise and fiercely loyal to the kingdom. She will be a fine ruler. Now if there aren't any objections, this is how we are going to proceed," Sir Igran looked about the room, some nodded, some grumbled, but no one protested. "Very well."

The assembly left and Igran went down from the great hall to the knight's quarters. He took the bedroll off his bunk and items from the chest at the foot of the bed.

"Are you sure about taking Frostford?" Orubark came down the stairs. "That is quite the undertaking."

"I think I can manage. Ragnar won't be too far away."

"That's true. But you could've also gone back to your homeland. The Lake Realm is a beautiful country. You could take the old keep in the foothills."

"I appreciate the thought," Igran closed his bag and threw it over his shoulder. "But I think I've moved on. Besides, I'm excited for something new. A good challenge is ahead."

"The West is rugged place. Those people may not want to be ruled by a loyalist."

"I'll do what I can," Igran walked to leave. "Till next time, Chief."

"Lord," Orubark nodded in return.

Igran shook his head and went up the stairs. The knights were talking with the princess and Myles.

"Are you leaving already?" Ragnar went over to him.

"Indeed. It's a long way to Frostford."

"I figured you would ride out with us," Ragnar gesture back to Alessia. "We won't be leaving though for a few days' time."

"No, I think I'll leave you two," Igran went to shake Ragnar's hand.

"I'll be seeing you around though. You know my hammer is there if you find yourself needing support."

"I'll call on you whenever I'm in need," Igran smiled and caught glimpse of Delwyn, talking with Myles. "Farewell, Ragnar," He turned and started walking down the hall. He passed the stone pillars and made it to the doors. He turned when he heard someone quickly approaching.

"You were just going to leave?" Delwyn asked. Igran sighed before responded.

"I think I'm going to miss you, lad. We put up some good fighting out there in the world."

"It'll be lonely traveling without you. I'd consider you a real mentor. And a good friend."

Igran smiled and embraced the young man.

"You're a brave man, Delwyn," He said. "I think you're dangerous enough to take this world."

As the months went by, refugees returned from the outer villages and worked to clean up their old capital. New banners were unfurled around the streets. The white and silver shined against the charcoal-toned rocks of the mountain, burned from the fire. Market stalls were reestablished, and traders even wandered back into the city.

Myles was working in a forge up by the palace. He pounded away on iron nails and tools. The fire kept him warm in the cold winter days as he worked constantly to keep up with the city trying to build itself again.

"I hope this world is not keeping so busy you forgot your personal obligations," Evangeline walked through the door.

"My lady," Myles bowed his head. "I hope your personal obligations have not kept you so busy that you forgot the world."

"Never," She kissed him. "Now come on. I told the soldiers I would have no one else escort me on my journey."

"Very well, your highness," Myles took off his apron and washed his face, then followed her outside. There was a carriage waiting on the road. Myles jogged ahead to open the door for her.

"Thank you, sire," She stepped in. Myles climbed up himself and sat on the bench next to her. The horse-drawn carriage rode down the streets of the castle. Villagers waved as it rode by, Evangeline waving out the thin windows. They exited under the main gate and turned to the road north.

"So, tell me again, where are we going?" Myles turned and asked. His breath cold be seen in the cold vehicle.

"You are my personal guard. It is not for you to know where we go, only that you are to protect me whatever may come."

"Is that how our marriage is going to work? We do not know where we are going, but only that we are to protect one another?"

"It seems like the only rational way," She smiled.

The carriage pulled them through the farmlands and the plains and brought them north of the Royal Plains into the Blackrock Bluffs. The wheels left two long tracks in the snow as they rolled over the hills and dipped through valleys. Herds of bison roamed the plains, their woolly fur dusted in ice. Their breath fogging the air around them.

Away from the herd and up the road from the carriage was a man standing on top of a hill. This man wore a white cloak and in his hands was a shovel. He was digging a hole underneath a lone tree.

"Stop the cart," Evangeline leaned forward and spoke to the driver through the window.

"Of course, my lady," He pulled back on the horse and the carriage came to a stop just down the hill from the man. The princess wrapped herself in her coat as she stepped out from the carriage, Myles quick to follow her. The man in white took out a sword and held it in his hands.

"Do not fight for yourself, but the one who is to come. Have faith in what you will not see until the setting sun. May Adonai be with you as he is with me. Always walk in the light and so may it be," Edwards said quietly as he gripped the hilt of the sword, the blade pointing down. He knelt and drove the blade into the rocky ground. A fresh mound of dirt lay before him. He took a step back from the sword, making a cross against the sky, and started to sing:

When we are weak, and the day has ended
When strivings cease and we are yet alone
The world may know they have still a watchman!
A guard, a savior on the throne

When comes the day we are poor in spirit
Who'll guide our way and fight for our side?
We shall not fear no arrows, snares, nor sword!
He is our fortress and our strength

He is our shield, his faithfulness our ramparts
When we bear his sword, he will crown us so
Have faith in God, who protects us through the fire
Bless Adonai, who gave us life through snow

"A song for the King?" Myles whispered.

"I don't think so…" Evangeline replied. "I've heard that name before though, Adonai. I heard my father mutter it sometimes."

"An ancestor, maybe?" Myles thought.

"No. I don't know who he is."

"Hmm, quite a name though."

"My lady," The carriage driver called. "We mustn't delay if you are to arrive on time."

"Very well," Evangeline turned held out her arm to be walked by Myles back to the cart. They drove off, leaving a trail of snow behind them as they continued across the Bluffs.

The man in a white cloak stayed on the hill, never noticing the two behind him.

"Goodbye, brother," Edwards said. From behind the hill, Joel, Amos, Willelm, and other men appeared. They were all in white cloaks.

"Let us press on," Willelm said. "There's much of the Realms yet to be covered."

Evangeline and Myles rode for a little while longer, dipping through the farmland, all covered in snow. Eventually, they came up to a walled vineyard. The trees and vines were all dressed and wrapped for the winter. Inside this vineyard was a tall stone building with a pointed roof and bell tower. No one was in sight.

"What is this place?" Myles looked around as they stepped out of the carriage.

"My father used to take us here. Sanctuary, it was called. There used to be a whole city here, but it was destroyed in the war. The ruins are probably under all this snow."

"I'm sorry."

"Don't be, what's important is still here," She walked toward the walls. From inside the monastery, came the sounds of singing and soft ringing of bells. Myles drew near to the gate, keeping a hand on the hilt of his sword. "You can relax. We're safe here. Now let's get out of this snow. They won't marry us from out here."

"Yes, ma'am," Myles pushed open the gate and walked Evangeline over to the temple. The inside of the stone building was decorated in lush garland with red and gold ribbons. Red berries popping from the greenery. Candles hung from the walls and filled the tall room with light. Snow blew lightly against the windows outside as the sun started to set. As they entered, an old man used his cane to stand from where he had been praying on the floor.

"Princess Evangeline, it has been many years since I have seen you," Ezemiah walked over to greet them.

"This is beautiful," She gasped.

"Fit for a queen," The old man smirked. "I assume this is the lucky man?"

"Yes sir," Myles bowed. His copper hair was brushed and hung down to his shoulders.

"It warms my heart to see you both in good health."

"It's been so long," The princess smiled.

"It has indeed. Lot has changed. I understand your father even changed the kingdom's colors to white and silver, purity and righteousness?" Ezemiah asked as he went to grab something off the side table.

"Yes," Evangeline said.

"Well then, you two shall be married in the same manner. In purity, ever pursing righteousness," He gave each of them a wreath crown to put on. A veil hung from the princess's and covered her face. He gave them also a pair of rings, that shone like Myles' sword. "Clothes of white and rings of silver. May they serve you a symbol of your marriage and a symbol of the kingdom you will lead."

"But we are not king and queen," Evangeline gently said.

"You will lead none the less. Shining examples in the Realms that will look dark for some time. But from you both, there will be a great light."

"We're honored by your words," She replied.

"Now, if there no grievances," Ezemiah continued. "Myles, do you promise to protect, defend, love, and serve your bride as long as you both shall live?"

"I do."

"Evangeline, do you promise to protect, defend, love, and serve your husband as long as you both shall live?"

"I do."

"Then I do pronounce you husband and wife. Lord and Lady of Castle Rock. May you live long and be blessed, the both of you."

Years went by and the empty streets of Castle Rock began to fill again. The desolate places now heard the sounds of men, orcs, elves, and dwarves, all at work in the city. The ruins were restored, and building built up again. The garden was brought back to life and plants started to grow again along the cliffs and streets. Towers once again reached up to the summits. And high on the peak of the mountain, in the palace was born a boy. News swept the castle and reached the entire kingdom. A price was born to Lady Evangeline and Lord Myles. The streets filled with singing and mirth. The lord knights from afar traveled to see the newborn King. The one who was named Adonai.

www.ingramcontent.com/pod-product-compliance
Lightning Source LLC
Chambersburg PA
CBHW031340020726
47499CB00005B/1349